STAND PROUD
and BARK

Sirius's Story from Puppy to Police K-9

A NOVEL
BY
Mark Enlow

BOOK OPENER PUBLISHING

Published by Book Opener Publishing, Phoenix, AZ, U.S.A.
bookopenerpublishing.com

First paperback edition, 2025

ISBN: 978-1-7357932-3-8 (paperback)
ISBN: 978-1-7357932-4-5 (e-book)

This book is dedicated to all past, present, and future, K-9 police dogs.

"Ode to a Dog"

The one who walks behind in humbleness,
always eager to accompany.

Alert and ready, willing to sacrifice to keep
one safe.

Never will this friend be proven ungrateful
or disloyal.

...and when all other worldly events have
gone awry it will remain steadfast in its
bond.

–Mark Enlow

ONE

I was the climber. Following the scent of milk, I could reach Mother's nutrient sources before my two sisters or brother could wag a tail. Although I hated to leave the warmth of my siblings huddled together bodies, I needed the nutrients Mother had to offer to grow big like her. She was my first hero.

Once my pink belly was full and extended, it was time for a nap, at least until Olivia emerged from the farmhouse to check on us. She always checks on us.

The next thing I remember is a firm grasp around my middle, followed by the coolness of a gentle Nebraska May breeze flowing easily through my thin puppy coat.

I heard Olivia's gentle voice. "You are too cute! You're not the biggest of the litter, but you're not the smallest either. You're my just right, little piggy!"

How embarrassing, Olivia. I'm a dog! A German shepherd! I squirmed in her grasp and wanted to be returned to the warmth of my pack. My eyes had finally opened yesterday, but I couldn't see her clearly yet.

Before she lowered me back to my family of snuggle butts she said. "What are we going to name you?" I know! You're always sniffing around, more than the others, and you sure can climb to the top of the heap. Let's call you, Sirius... and your sweet brother, Nova... and your sisters, Celeste and Calypso!"

Sounds good! Now can I get back to naptime. I have to pee! If I pee right now, I know I won't be named after a heavenly star.

She kissed me on the nose and placed me back in the middle of my nice, warm family.

I watched with my blurry vision as she picked up each of my siblings, examining them carefully, told them their new names, and then placed them back in the group.

Mother watched with a keen interest until all her pups were back in her care.

Olivia left some food and water in Mother's bowls and trudged back inside.

I felt secure in my little world that is until my eyes started to focus on some things around me. There was a white corral fence that surrounded us and the farmhouse. Someone, probably Olivia, had nailed chicken wire to it to keep us in and safe, but also to keep any bothersome dangerous critters out.

Late one night, I was jostled out of a deep sleep by Mother's growl. I had only heard her growl once so I knew something was amiss.

Mother stood up and sniffed the air. She growled longer and deeper next, then barked. Her tail stood straight out. I raised by head to look in the direction that she pointed to. It was towards the gate. With the help of the moonlight, I could make out two glowing eyes affixed to a silhouette. It wasn't the shape of anything that I had seen before in my brief eight weeks on earth. The shadow with the pointed ears and long, wide tail crept towards us.

In four large bounds Mother was on top of the intruder. Dust flew all around her. The sleek shadow darted back outside the fence through a small gap between the gate and its mooring post. The light came on Olivia's front porch and she came running.

"What's going on? I heard the barking." Olivia noticed the disturbed dust and set of tracks by the gate. "It was that coyote again, wasn't it? I lost too many chicks to him! Now that I see where he is squeezing through the fence, I'll fix that tomorrow. In the meantime, everyone follow me to the house. I'll gather some covers together and put them in the spare bedroom for you tonight."

It was nice in the house and darker without the moon. Except I really missed hearing the crickets and the smell of the hay in our farm shed. It's just for one night. I hoped.

The next day after Olivia fixed the fence, we went on our first expedition, to a lake nearby. Monty, who also lived in the farmhouse, joined us. We didn't see much of him around the house since he kept busy trying to make a go of it, running the farm, most of the time single-handedly.

The short truck ride in the back seat was bumpy and fun. I could smell Mother in the back cargo area so I felt secure with her presence. After a large bump I pretended to fall over on my brother and we got into a wrestling match. At the next big bump the fun started all over again.

I never heard Monty and Olivia laugh so much.

My sisters just huddled together and slept in the far-left corner of the backseat. I don't know how they could sleep with all of our squeals and squirming, especially my big brother's extra loud squeals. I call him my big brother because, well... he's bigger than me and he was born first in the litter.

I soon smelled something different in the air, like pine and water mixed together. The bouncing soon stopped and the back side door opened.

The first thing I saw was Olivia smiling at us.

"Come on girls and boys, let's go check out the lake!"

When she stepped aside, I gawked at the most water I had ever seen.

Monty opened the truck's back tailgate and let Mother jump out.

Before us pups could get our bearings, Olivia ran for the lake at full speed, stopping at the lake's edge. She was pretty fast, but not as quick as I've seen Mother run before.

Next, I saw Olivia run onto an old dock, she paused at its edge, then she kind of fell in the lake. Part of that old dock went with her. I know it wasn't a jump because I practice jumps all day.

Monty was trying to keep us rowdy ones together and guide us towards the lake when Mother saw Olivia disappear from sight. I said Mother could really move, but everyone else should now address her as Bullet. She reached the dock and leapt off before Monty could yell out, Oliva!

Monty sprinted for the lake, but he wasn't that fast, because I was right behind him, short legs and all. I didn't see Olivia resurface. I knew this was bad, like when I got my first bath and ducked my head underwater and couldn't breathe.

By the time Monty reached the dock, bubbles sprang up from the water's surface followed by Mother. Olivia emerged next, clutching the back of Mother's neck as she gasped for air.

Monty dove in and together the three made the short swim to shore where the other pups continued to frolic along the water's edge.

I knew I had one of Mother's personality traits and demonstrated it, when I dove off the dock and tried to catch up with the rescue.

I had gotten all four paws moving and was starting to move forward towards the shore. I thought I had this when my large pink belly, full of milk, sank me. It was blurry down there. Reminded me of the first time that I was able to focus a few weeks ago. I kept my paws churning and managed to resurface for a brief moment only to start to sink again. I had caught a glimpse of mother rapidly swimming towards me on my resurface. The water churned around her, I hoped it wouldn't be my last vision of her.

I felt a tight sharp grip on the back of my neck. I was back above the water, safely held in Mother's mouth. We reached the shore just as Olivia was able to sit up.

"Good work!" Monty told Mother. "Two rescues in one day!"

After resting a bit, I joined my brother and sisters scampering along the shore.

"Monty that old dock almost did me in!" Olivia winced. "When it gave way, I smacked my head on a piece of it that broke off in the water."

Monty felt her head. "Nice sized goose egg! We'll just keep an eye on you for the next few hours. How are you feeling?   Any wooziness?"

"Nah, I'm just thankful for that dog."

Monty smiled and asked, "Which one?"

"You're right." Olivia replied. "Sirius tried to help. Such a brave pup!"

As they watched the little dogs frolic, Olivia said, "All of these precious pups are going to fill special places and needs—too soon I'm afraid. We're going to really miss them."

TWO

I liked the training in the farmyard. Olivia taught us some cool tricks like sitting, paw high-fives, how to walk on a leash without giving into the notion of chasing a few chickens and a lot of other stuff.

The best chicken chaser was Celeste. She always got her chicken, but Olivia taught all of us to catch and release. No harm done, but a lot of fun. After all, you could only wrestle with your siblings for so long before they got a little snippy.

All of us were getting bigger except Calypso. Well, she had gotten a little larger, but she was the runt of the litter. ...and you know what? She soon secured the shotgun seat next to Olivia when we went into town. I was envious, but she's a good kid. Well worth a lick or two.

The big trips to the pet warehouse store always ended in a lot of bags taking up our space in the back. I sniffed every crease in those sacks and determined that they were worth taking up space. There was food in them along with some treats that I fought hard to keep Nova out of. But could I keep him out of them? No, so I helped him eat the evidence. Clever of me.

Olivia always brought the empty wrappers to our attention when we got home. I think she intently left some tasty morsels for us to find. She always laughed about it and gave each of us a good pet and a scratch behind the ears afterwards.

One thing though... I was raring to go anyplace as long as it wasn't the place we went to when I was younger. They called it the vets. It's hard to speak of even now. The place was full of strange smells. Not food, but stuff you knew to stay out of. Oh— a lot of other dogs, all kinds, paced around looking for the closest door to escape from.

We waited in that place for dog years. A young girl with some kind of rope around her neck—she must've been the local people pack leader, led us to a small room and shut the door behind us.

I was okay but, my sister, Calypso was shivering. I licked her and smelled her muzzle trying to calm her down. It was working until the people pack leader lifted her way up onto a table. Another man came into the room. He had a rope around his neck, too. He was dressed like the ice cream man that I had seen in town once.

Now I was worried and confused. We had been taught by Olivia not to jump on any furniture especially tables. For that was the place where we very intently watched our masters consume food. Now, Calypso was on a table. I growled.

"Sirius, stop that, right this instant!" Olivia demanded. "It's okay. She not going to hurt her."

I sat down, unable to see what was going on. We each took a turn on the table in the sky except me.

Then... it was my turn.

I endured what my fellow siblings had been subjected to. First, the ice cream man shoved a stick up my butt while the girl held my head and tried to sweet-talk me. That lasted for an eternity until the stick beeped. He pulled it out, looked at it and said, "Looks normal, good boy!"

Next, he looked in my eyes and ears. He kind of poked and prodded me in a few spots. Then he stuck the ends of his rope in his ears. He felt around my middle, before placing a shiny little bowl that was attached to the other end of the rope on my chest. The room grew quiet. I could hear what he heard. I didn't need a rope with a bowl. Thump... thump... thump. Wow, I had no idea I made the same sound that resonated from every living thing I had met so far in my brief life. I was so excited that I growled softly.

"Sirius, remember, no growling." Olivia reminded me.

I looked up at her and gave her the puppy-eye, the have pity on me expression. I wasn't growling... just excited about my new heartbeat.

The girl handled the man something pointed, but before I could growl, I felt two slight pinches topside.

"You have some beautiful pups, Miss!" He lowered me to the floor.

"Thank you, Doc!" Olivia replied. "They are one fantastic, diverse litter."

Calypso pawed at the closed door while Nova raised up on his back paws and gave the door a good shove with his front paws. We were ready to get out of here.

As Olivia drove all of us home, we fell asleep, even that spoiled Calypso in the front seat.

THREE

Olivia spread a big, soft blanket on her living room floor and we all hopped on. This happened one other time for our 6-month birthdays and it had ended with cake and ice cream.

Umm! We were waiting, as patiently as any salivating 10-month-old pups could and we even stayed on the blanket. I was proud of my brother and sister's patience. They had been paying attention in training after all.

Well.... Here comes Olivia carrying a small birthday cake along with some ice cream. All of us could smell its sugary sweetness when Olivia first brought it into the house. We acted surprised.

Olivia sat the goodies on a small table next to us and stuck one candle in the cake. She set the cake on fire while she started to sing a song that we had heard before.

It was so embarrassing, my brother, Nova started howling, and Calypso joined in. Celeste and I just looked at each other. We knew that they wouldn't shut up until Olivia stopped singing and applauded.

When the delicious cake and ice cream was served, I finished mine first, then helped Celeste finish hers. It was the least I could do since she didn't howl with the other two. Besides, the sweet edibles were scrumptious!

The next day we had some visitors. A van drove up to the farmhouse gate and the side door slid open. Kids—we had kids visiting, yea! Let the games begin! First off was a handsome boy in a chair with wheels followed by four other children.

They were placed one-at-a-time by two adults onto a platform attached to the van. It would lower to the ground and then raise back to where it started. Maybe if they think I'm cute enough they'll let me ride it! Although, I think not, since we were getting close to adult size and just a little of our cute puppy-ness had waned. Just a little bit mind you, maybe...

Olivia commanded us to stay, then she let them in the gate. When all of the kids were gathered together in the shade, Olivia called us one by one to see the children close up. I followed last after Calypso.

I was losing my patience. It was my turn. Calypso, the front seat hog was lingering with every child and every kid was paying her compliments. Huh! Don't scratch her behind her ears or she will never leave, I wanted to howl!

Finally, Olivia said, "Okay, Calypso, girl, time to move on. Come here!" Calypso trotted over to Olivia's side.

My turn! I walked slowly up to the first child, so as not to scare him and received the best head scratch ever.

The dark-haired boy said to me, "You're a good dog, aren't you boy?"

I answered by placing my head on his knee.

"Ah, you're a sweet pup, too!" He said.

I wanted to keep this one. Maybe invite him to our next blanket party! I could give him Calypso's cake share. A doggie grin spread across my muzzle.

I moved down the line, stopping to give a sniff and a lick or two to each child. I was well rewarded with pets and head rubs.

After the introductions, each kid got a turn at throwing a ball for us to fetch. Remember Celeste, the ultimate chicken chaser, well... she was also the fastest ball returner. She was a fast flash, that girl!

The two adults and Olivia were talking and I heard one of the visitors say, "I think all of your shepherd's would be an asset to any of our children, but I know we have to choose one. So, based on our observations, we like Calypso. What do you think?"

"I agree with your choice. I'll miss her, of course. But I know she'll have a good home and help a child live a normal life." Olivia said.

Calypso received a rousing early morning send-off the next day of nips, sniffs, licks from us, and lots of hugs by Olivia. She boarded the van that we had seen yesterday, bound for children's mobility assistance training and a new, rewarding life. I miss her already.

FOUR

On a cold day in mid-winter, Olivia and Monty took me to a construction zone and then to a shooting range. I wasn't sure why? Both were really loud, but I soon became used to the constant noise. Olivia didn't do any construction work or shoot any guns at these places. I liked the different activities at both though and got a lot of pets and friendly comments from both camps.

That's when it happened! We were strolling along the street bordering the side where a huge construction crane was lifting some pallets. A man in a blue uniform and a vested dog on a leash walked by and stopped to chat.

"That's a fine-looking shepherd that you have there, Miss." he stated.

"Thank you, your shepherd is quite the handsome one as well," Olivia replied. "Can I pet him, Corporal?"

"Oh sure, he's a gentle giant," he smiled. "My name's Tom Harper and this here is Jacob. Jacob is as sweet as they come, always waiting for me to give him a job to do."

She stroked the dog's head and scratched him behind his ear. "I'm Olivia and this is Sirius. We're pleased to meet you."

"Same here," Tom replied.

I was getting jealous. Stop petting that dog, Olivia! How dare a strange dog get such attention! Then I remembered that Olivia treated every dog we met as her own. I relaxed.

The man in blue reached down and gave me a pet, too and a rub behind my ear. Ah, it does pay to remain cool!

Jacob and I sniffed each other over and we both decided to be friends after a few tail wags.

"The police K-9 vest, is it bullet proof?" Olivia asked.

"Yep. The department finally found it in their budget and hearts to outfit all of our dogs. The dogs are police officers same as us," he answered.

"Here." He handed her a card with his division and contact information on it. "The department is looking for a few good dogs to join our ranks, if you know of any, give us a call. I'm actually the one that gives the new recruits their K-9 temperament test, to see if they might pass training and fit in."

"I've raised service dogs and search and rescue K-9's for a lot of different organizations. I'll keep it in mind. Thanks, great to meet you." She tucked the card in her pocket.

"Same here, you have a fantastic day." He smiled and passed by.

Well, I thought if anyone of us deserves a cool, prestigious job like that, it was Nova. Besides he was the largest of our pack and probably the most powerful as far as dominance goes. Still. I really admired the dark-blue, gold lettered K-9 police vest that my new friend, Jacob wore. Something I could howl about given the chance.

When we got home my sister and brother greeted us like usual, as if we had been gone for weeks. They must have gotten it from me as I did the same thing only I was worse, I wagged my whole body.

With Mother watching intently, Celeste got Nova and I started on a feather-flying chicken round-up. That eventually led us to our tongues hanging on the ground and a sweet nap in the lean-to hay bin. All of us were exhausted.

A couple of days later, Monty took an unusual day off from farming and introduced us to a new game. Olivia herded all of us inside the house while Monty stayed outside. When Olivia finally let us out I saw that there were Styrofoam, paper, and ceramic cups turned upside down and scattered around the farmyard. Monty held up a small, square piece of cloth for each of us to sniff. After each of us got a good whiff, Monty said, "Find!"

We had done some hide-and-seek games before, but this was a new one with a twist. Nova took off first, sniffing at every cup he found. Celeste was right behind him, followed by me. We hadn't detected anything under the cups so far, that's when Celeste ran past Nova to the next cup closest to Nova's position. Well, Nova didn't agree with that one bit. He bounded over to Celeste, pushed her aside to sniff the cup firsthand. He found nothing.

Celeste ignored him and just moved on to the next closest cup and continued her search.

I was covering some other targets on the far side of the yard trying to stay out of Nova's way. I was confident that I was on the right track, because I was following Monty's recent footstep scents.

Monty and Olivia watched with great interest from the sidelines, then I heard Monty shout, "Nova, here!"

My brother had knocked over one of the paper cups in his haste instantly disqualifying him from the game. Now it was just me and Celeste.

Olivia turned to Monty and said, "I think Sirius is tracking the strength of your scent trying to find where you might have paused long enough to hide the cloth swatch. Look, see! He's even skipping some of the cups with his nose on the prize. Sirius is a good tracker!"

"We'll see," Monty answered. "It sure looks that way."

I caught a few words of what she said as I sniffed closer to the farmyard gate. I heard two words, 'Sirius' and 'good'. I knew then that I was on the right track. Ah... the trail ended at the gate. I jumped once at the metal gate and it clanged against its mooring post. I sat down and waited for assistance.

Monty came walking over and swung the gate wide open.

Celeste paused to watch the goings-on, but resumed her cup to cup search.

Monty's trail led to the barn. I pawed the door and waited for Monty. When he opened it, I kept my nose down next to the hay-covered dirt floor. My tail stood straight out. The scent grew stronger, as I sniffed my way to a small mound of hay, back in a stall. I sniffed and gently pawed the hay away revealing a ceramic upside down cup. I barked and sat.

Monty ran over and picked up the cup. "Good boy, Sirius! You did it. Nice job!"

I watched him hold up the cloth swatch for me to see and sniff. Whenever I heard my name and 'good' in the same sentence I always wanted to do a backflip, but I figured I would probably hurt myself. A doggie-smile would have to suffice.

FIVE

I was starting to pant more outside as the weather started to turn warmer again. When it was really cold outside the last few months, a lot of visitors had come through the gate. I was a member of the welcoming committee along with Celeste and Nova. We always tried to out-wag each other. I think my full-body wag won mostly, but that's a tail wagging opinion.

They usually pulled up in vans with some kind of, what looked like, graffiti painted on the doors. All of them were sniffed and checked-in before they were allowed passage. We always waited in anticipation of the next guest because we received some fantastic pets and ear scratches. I regarded all of them as dog people.

One day, another van pulled up and a woman with a tall boy with sunglasses and a cane got out, then proceeded to the gate.

The woman smelled like flowers. She asked, "Well, are you pups going to let us in?"

That's all it took for an instant body-wag.

She undid the fence latch and came through the gate.

Both were checked in by Celeste and me.

The boy had a youngster smell, kind of like puppies have a newness smell. Nova must have liked it a lot because he kept nuzzling the boy's hand and pants leg. The boy felt Nova's ears and smiled. He slowly moved both his hands over Nova from tip to tail. Nova stood still, enjoying the attention. When the boy's curiosity was satisfied he gave Nova a head rub and even gave Nova a hug.

Nova had completely ignored the woman. Which wasn't at all like him. He always had to sniff anyone who was near. I made up for his rudeness by giving her a good second sniffing and found that I liked her earthy garden scent.

Celeste just stood around and wagged her tail.

Mother stood back and just watched us mostly now-a-days, but just knowing she was nearby was enough for us.

Our two new friends proceeded to the farmhouse door and were greeted and let in by Olivia.

Monty came out of the house just as a game of 'chase each other' ended, which Celeste had started. Celeste won as usual. Nova and I called it a tie.

Monty put a collar and leash on Nova and walked him back inside the house. It was strange seeing Nova tug Monty towards the house though. None of us had done that for months. We were trained well. Nova just wanted to see the boy again, no doubt about it!

Mother, Celeste, and I just laid around a bit, keeping an eye on the porch door. Finally, the door opened and Nova came running out towards us. The woman and boy emerged next followed by Olivia and Monty. The woman held Nova's leash and collar though.

We all stood, tails wagging, as Nova reached us. He was acting strange, even for Nova. He sniffed all three of us, did a nose muzzle kiss, and then rejoined the side of the woman and boy.

Olivia petted Nova and said, "Guys I have an announcement to make. I'm sad to say that Nova will be leaving us. However, I'm happy to say that he'll be going to training, to be a guide dog for the visually challenged!"

Nova wagged his tail, and the boy and woman smiled.

Well... Mother, Celeste, and I knew it already. We always felt that Nova and Calypso were destined to do great things. Dogs have a way of sensing the moment at hand, too. Call it a sixth sense, maybe, or intuition. But it is what makes us the beneficial caregivers that we are.

SIX

On the day Nova left, Monty noticed that Olivia looked a little down early in the afternoon. "Hey, let's take a hike through the mountain pass. What do you think, Liv?" He asked.

"I thought you said you had plowing to do for the cabbage crop?" Olivia answered. "It would be nice to get out of here for a few hours. Maybe, take the dogs. I already miss Nova."

"Me, too," Monty nodded. "The plowing and planting can wait until tomorrow. Let's go! I'll get the dogs gear together."

Olivia sped down the hall and pulled on some hiking boots and a light jacket and raced back. "Hey, don't forget your jacket and boots, Sweetie!"

"Got em," Monty replied. They headed out the door and rounded up the pack.

When the dirt road met concrete they headed the four-wheel SUV east on Interstate 80.

Celeste and I curled up with Mother and took a together nap on a blanket in the back cargo area.

When the SUV's tires hit the dirt park road, I jumped up. How can Celeste sleep through this? I jumped on her and she growled. She's up! Alright! Get ready sister to see one of my favorite places again! Smell the pine! I put my snoot out the open window space. Ah... smell that air! There's a lot of other animal friends close by today!

Mother arose when they came to a stop in a small cut-out area in the forest.

Olivia and Monty jumped out and we waited for the tailgate to open. Ever have a moment while you were waiting for something to happen and had a random thought. I wondered if they named the back SUV door in honor of dogs. Tailgate—huh... Well maybe... not... Strange stuff! I probably had too many carrots for lunch.

Once we had our leashes on, Mother and Celeste walked with Monty, and Olivia and I dominated the led position.

Our tails wagged for the first mile then we got warm and just panted after that. I could smell an opossum nearby and I paused for a moment to see if Olivia would let me loose for an investigation. She held firmly to the lease so I moved on.

We came to a little creek that I had heard gurgling, ten minutes before we got there.

Olivia and I took the lead again. We walked side by side until the trail lined with boulders squeezed us to a single-file march. Now I had the pack leader position alone!

"I think we should turn around soon, Liv," Monty said. "It'll be dark in about three hours."

"Yep, I think so," Olivia answered. "When it gets dark up here its three shades of night. That's for sure."

"There's a clearing ahead. We can turn around there, Liv."

Olivia did a slight stumble on a trail tree root, but recovered and replied, "Okay."

I smelled something I had caught whiffs of before, up here in the mountains, except this was close-by.

We rounded a blind corner that opened to the clearing and the smell smacked me right in the muzzle. In the center of the clearing, foraging on a berry bush, was a large, black bear. She had two pups with her about my size.

"Uh-oh!" Olivia declared.

"Start backing up slowly!" Monty said in a calm yet firm tone.

The bear was looking our way. Her cubs gathered behind her.

Celeste started a barking frenzy.

That's when the bear charged.

Fifty yards remained between us. It was closing-in on us fast.

Monty and Olivia while still holding on to our leashes waved their arms above their heads trying to look bigger.

But the mother bear continued her advance towards us.

Mother took a powerful leap forward, causing Monty to lose a grip on her leash. She headed straight for the bear.

It halted when Mother charged. The bear raised itself upward, ready to pounce, its sharp claws at the ready.

Mother was smart. She knew that even she was no match for a bear like this one. She darted pass the huge bear just out of reach and headed towards the two cubs.

Monty, Olivia, and I stood still unsure of what to do next.

I saw the large bear spin back around and charge towards Mother in an attempt to protect her cubs.

I had to do something, but what? I'm just a dog! She's a really big bear! Mother! Panic flashed through my brain!

So, I leapt forward and the leash went tight causing me to choke and cough, then the pull from my restraint stopped. I was free!

I reached the bear a moment before it was on mother. The bear took one huge paw and swatted the right side of my body. I went into an intense pain spasm. I could see white streaks of light and nothing else for a moment.

I rolled uncontrollably and thought the spill would never end. I finally came to rest in some bushes alongside the clearing. I couldn't move. I waited for it to finish the attack. I heard Mother's rapid barking and then everything went black.

When I awoke, a steady bright light blinded my eyes for a few minutes.

Must be in doggy heaven I thought. I didn't feel pain any longer. I heard Olivia say, "Sirius, Sirius..."

Olivia was here, too. I was happy that she was with me, but angry that my crazed heroics hadn't saved her. I wondered about Mother, Monty, and Celeste.

I heard Olivia say, "Sirius, you're awake. You're going to be okay. You're at the vet's, sweetie."

Oh! That's what this place is! I was lying on my side and tried to raise my head, but my neck was stiff and I was groggy.

I heard Monty say, "Sirius, you're a hero. You saved all of us today. Just rest. Everyone's okay thanks to you."

No, I thought, Mother is the hero.

I heard the vet say, "The x-rays show three fractured ribs and he has a concussion along with some contusions of course. Did I heard my assistant say he got hit by a car?"

"No," Olivia stated. "He got hit by a bear. A large, black bear who was with her cubs.

"Lucky to be alive, I'd say," Doc Samuel answered. "He just needs some rest now. I want to keep him here for observation. I'll give you a call in the morning to let you know how he's doing. With any luck he might be able to go home in a day or two."

"Your right, doc," Monty agreed. "Could've been a lot worse."

"That's for sure! Thanks doc!" Olivia said.

Olivia gave me a light ear scratch and a kiss on the muzzle.

I saw a real hero today, Mother. She always was one, even before today—especially to me. I drifted off back to sleep.

SEVEN

Olivia's cell phone rang a top 80's tune before sunrise. It was 6:15am. Olivia cleared her throat and picked up her phone on the fourth note.

"Hello."

"Hello, Olivia, this is Doc Samuel at the animal hospital."

"Hi, Doc. How is Sirius?"

"He's doing better. My assistant took Sirius for a slow walk around the office. He did alright, but I can see considerable stiffness in his gait. Perfectly normal after such a trauma. I'd like to keep him here for one more day and give him an IV, to get his strength up."

"Alright. We'll pick him up tomorrow, then?"

"That would be fine. We'll take good care of him."

"Thanks, Doc, and I just want you to know how much I appreciate the help that you've given me and my dogs over the years."

"Olivia, I know it's not easy breeding and raising service dogs. I'm sure there are plenty of people out there that would like to thank you."

"Thank you, Doc. See you, tomorrow. Bye."

"See you then, bye."

Olivia immediately dialed Monty with the news. He had headed out for some early sunrise plowing.

Monty paused the John Deere tractor and

grabbed his phone. A smile spread across Monty's face as Olivia relayed the good news.

"Great, fantastic...!" he exclaimed. "Sirius is one brave-hearted dog! That's for sure. I'll be back at the house by 11 to meet with the people from the therapy organization."

"Okay, sounds good" she answered. "One thing though. When Sirius arrives home tomorrow, he's going to look for Celeste-I mean... he's going to miss her, don't you think? Should we postpone the pick up today?"

"It's too late to postpone," he said. "The trainers are flying in from San Francisco. Besides, it would be too much excitement for Sirius if he were home. I know what you're saying though. I feel badly for him especially after all he's been through."

"Me, too," she replied sadly.

"He's a tough boy with a big heart. He'll be okay, Liv." His Mother will be there to greet him."

"Hey..." "She's been looking for him, too!" she replied.

"She has?" Monty asked. "I'm not surprised. They're super close."

"Yeah... they are that," she agreed. "Okay, see you in a bit, Monty. Get that field furrowed! Bye."

"Bye, Liv."

Monty returned home just in time to shower and change out of his coveralls before greeting two people who had just arrived at the outside gate.

"Hello, welcome to the farm!" I'm Monty."

The older man and a younger woman replied in a chorus, "thank you!" The older gentleman chuckled and said, "My assistant and I have been doing voice choreographing ever since she became my assistant. I'm Frank Dobbins and this is Mia Parker. Pleased to meet you."

"I can identify with that," Monty agreed and smiled. "My wife, Olivia and I have been doing that since we met.

"Please," he opened the gate and motioned towards the house, "right this way."

When they arrived on the front porch, a few barks resounded from inside the house.

"Let me go inside and bring out Celeste and her mother." Monty stated. "Be right back."

He went inside and had Celeste and her Mother sit side by side on the hall rug. "Stay!" He extended his arm out like a crossing guard stopping traffic.

Olivia stood at the other end of the hall and watched.

Monty opened the front door.

The dog's tails wagged like a symphony conductor's baton in a fast tempo, however they both stayed put on the hall rug.

"My, what well behaved and charming hosts we have here." Frank said with a wide smile.

"Okay... good girls." Monty said. He patted both on the head and coaxed both of them forward.

Mia stooped down to greet them both and received dog kisses from both. "You two are so adorable, why Celeste looks just like her mother, no wonder."

Frank stroked the top of their heads, then asked each for a paw shake, gesturing for Mother's paw first. As soon as he did, Celeste raised her paw at the same time.

"How cute is that?" Mia stated.

With Mother's paw in his right hand, Frank took Celeste's paw in his left hand and gently shook both their paws. Pleased to meet you both, very pleased!" I see someone has been doing a lot of training perhaps."

Frank looked at Monty.

"No, not me. Olivia is the trainer. I'm just a helper, thank you."

"Olivia, you can be very proud of these dogs," Frank surmised. "I'm sure of it. Celeste is going to make a fine therapy dog. She'll probably be certified in record time. She'll provide a lot of hope and encouragement to folks in hospitals nursing homes and rehabilitation centers.

"She will shine, no doubt." Mia added.

"Thank you, both." Olivia said.

"By the way, Olivia," Frank said, "the last dog that you raised from a pup for us is one of our brightest stars when she's on a therapy visit. She truly is and you aptly named her, Star—a fitting name indeed."

"Thank you. Won't you both come in and stay for lunch?"

"Thank you, but I have a flight to catch in a few hours. Mia will be driving back to our center with Celeste. I make it a rule that we never transport dogs in an airline cargo hold. I believe in treating dogs like I would want to be treated and a storage area under a plane's belly with luggage is not for me either."

Olivia, Monty, and Mother escorted Frank, Mia, and Celeste to the gate.

"We appreciate the hospitality. Thank you both for everything." Frank said.

Your welcome." Olivia replied.

"Thank you, we'll take good care of her." Mia said.

"You're welcome. You both have a safe trip."

Olivia, Monty, and Mother after using up all of their goodbyes, turned and headed back to the house.

EIGHT

Hospital food was yuck and I wanted to go home now. I ached when I moved too fast, but the doc's assistant let me linger long enough on our hospital interior walks to satisfy me. I met a three-legged rabbit, a turtle with a broken shell, a cat with a scruffy coat, and plenty of other brothers and sisters with various maladies. I felt gratitude for actual being alive and compassion for others.

When I saw Olivia and Monty peering into my kennel cage I yapped with joy. That hurt my tender ribs, but I didn't care, I was going home!

Olivia took me out with my leash to the SUV while Monty made peace with the front desk. Mother was in the backseat! I kissed her until she sneezed, then took a seat next to one of the windows.

Monty put the windows down enough to let in some flower-laden fresh air. I was in heaven.

On the dirt part of the road near home, Monty drove slower than usual to avoid the bumps and bounces.

When we arrived inside the farmyard and I searched the area for Celeste.

Olivia's mouth turned down. "Look, ah... he's looking for Celeste, oh..."

Monty nodded his head in agreement. "I'm not

surprised that it's the first thing he would do."

I found two new scents on the front porch and traced them back to the gate. Celeste's fresh scent followed along with them. I knew what happened... she had gone with them. I lowered my head and tail in a tribute to my little sister.

"Ah, Sirius, pup... Celeste has left to be a therapy dog," Olivia said softly. "She went to help others like you did up on that mountain, and when you jumped in that lake to save me even though you were too young to swim."

She raised my head and held it between her hands, then she put her nose next to mine.

I looked into her eyes and saw a deep kindness that I had always sensed from her.

"One day, maybe we can have a family reunion here at the farm, boy... Wouldn't that be great?" She asked.

I just knew, deep in my heart that my brother and two sisters were gone and they wouldn't be coming back. Puppyhood ended for me that day. I wagged my tail once just so Olivia would feel better and walked toward the house.

In the next few weeks I regained my strength and the aches and pains finally subsided. Mother was starting to show a little gray around her muzzle, but that didn't stop her from playing in a fun game of 'who can tear this ball to shreds first' game.

She won. I let her. She was my Mother.

NINE

I felt that my time on the farm also would soon end. I called it a dog's intuition. There was a yearning deep inside me. I had a calling like my brothers and sisters before me.

I would miss Mother. She was the only dog before us pups arrived and she would be the only dog when I left. However, she had Olivia and Monty, and chickens to chase, so I knew that she would be alright.

I laid in the hay-filled lean-to pondering what my destiny might be when Officer Tom Harper showed up at the gate. I barked a greeting and ran over to see him.

"Well, there you are Sirius! How are you, boy?" he asked.

Olivia walked off the porch and headed for the gate. "Hi, Tom!"

"Hey Olivia, I see you have a guard dog."

"Yea, he's a good intruder alarm, that's for sure." She unfastened the gate. "Please come in."

"Thanks," he said while reaching down and giving me several pets and strokes on my head. "Hey, Sirius, you look good! I heard about your bear encounter. You are one brave dog!"

I was really warming up to this guy. My tail wagged faster as he spoke.

I wondered where Jacob, his partner was.

"Jacob is in the back seat of the cruiser," Tom stated as if he had read my thoughts. "Would you like to see him, Sirius?" he asked.

My tail wagged faster and I nudged him with my nose.

"Okay." Tom walked to the back car door and let Jacob out.

I noticed that he didn't have his police K-9 vest on and he now looked just like any other dog.

Jacob ran over and we sniff-greeted each other. A moment later, we were running around the farm yard like it was old home week before settling on the shaded front porch to watch the chickens roam. Mother padded onto the porch from the house's open door and walked over to us. She eyed and sniffed Jacob then settled down to join us.

Olivia, Monty, and Tom decided to perch on the porch, too. I knew why. Because it was the type of spring day when you could lie on a grassy knoll with your paws skyward and contemplate what each cloud reminded you of.

Tom handed Olivia a new contact card. Here's new information to contact me directly."

"I've been promoted to sergeant and reassigned. I'm now in charge of overseeing K-9 training for the dogs and their handlers.

"Congratulations! Sergeant!" Olivia exclaimed.

"Congrats, Tom!" Monty added. "Does this mean that you won't be giving Sirius his temperament test?"

"The promotion took effect last month, but I'll still be the evaluator on this one. Officer Rose

Garcia will be the handler. She is one of our best K-9 handlers. I think Sirius is a special dog."

I wagged my tail upon hearing my name mentioned. Jacob took the hint and wagged a few times, too.

"Look at those two, would you?" Monty observed. "They're like two peas in a pod."

"They seem to like each other's company," Olivia said.

"No doubt," Tom nodded.

"Depending on how Sirius's tests come out, Sirius could be a dual-purpose K-9, "Tom stated.

"What exactly does that mean?" Monty questioned.

"It's elite. It means he could be a patrol canine doing duties such as officer protection, search and rescue, tracking, criminal apprehension, or evidence searches. But, he could also be specialized in the detection of narcotics or maybe explosives as a second specialty."

"Impressive!" Olivia said.

"It is," Tom agreed "...and well needed in our department. Right now we only have two other dual K-9's. Jacob's one of them. His other specialty is narcotics detection."

"That would be special!" Olivia replied. "Would you like a glass of fresh squeezed lemonade, Tom? Monty?"

"Thanks," Tom said. "I'd love one."

"Me, too, Sweetie. Do you need some help bringing them out, Olivia?" Monty asked.

"I've got it, thanks. You stay here and keep Tom

company." She stood and walked inside.

"Tom, has the department ever lost a K-9, I mean in the line of duty?"

"Unfortunately, yes. A year ago, we lost one of our officer dogs while tracking a bank robbery suspect. He was shot by the suspect."

"Oh... Sorry to hear that. You said officer dogs..."

"All of our canines are referred to as officers. They are one of us. They all have ID cards and badges and all are now equipped with flak jackets, thanks to a pet warehouse's donation."

"Glad to hear they have protective vests now," Monty nodded.

Olivia pushed open the porch screen door carrying a tray with three tall, sweating glasses of lemonade and a plate of ginger snaps. "Did I miss something? Did I hear a mention of protective vests?"

"Ah... yeah," Tom answered. "I was just telling Monty about a dog we lost in a bank robber pursuit. We lost one of our own when our K-9 caught up with the suspect in a dead-end alley. He had him cornered. Just a few seconds before officers on foot arrived, the suspect pulled out a revolver."

"Oh... poor dog... so the dogs have protective vests now?" she asked.

"Yes... and I wish we had them back then. Everyone in the police department took it as a personal loss. The K-9, Maxim, has a memorial plague with his picture on it. It's displayed where our other officers that were killed in the line-of-duty are memorialized. It's in the main entrance lobby at our headquarters building."

"That's so sad," Olivia stated.

"One thing about Sirius, though. I'm glad that dogs don't have to go through a background check." Olivia laughed.

Sirius's ears perked up when he heard his name.

"Uh-huh," Olivia said, gazing at Sirius, "...and those were my favorite slippers, too," Olivia chuckled.

I lowered my head and sighed.

Tom, Monty, and Olivia laughed.

"It's okay, I still love you," Olivia said.

Whew, that's a relief! I thought.

Tom laughed. "Our K-9 candidates are, if you'll excuse the expression, vetted by their temperament, drive, dominance, and obedience. They need to have ambition and been eager to please the handler. They have to have an even keel in the personality department and be dominant, but not too dominant to control. They're special!" He smiled.

"They are and Sirius is, too," Monty said.

"I believe you're correct," Tom replied. "Sirius will be the first dog placed in a new program that I've developed. He'll reside with the officer who will be his future handler as both Sirius and the officer undergo separate training programs.

Then after the initial separate training they'll train together as a team. Before, the dog wasn't assigned to an officer until after training. We had a study done that showed that the additional bonding of residing with the dog's future handler enhanced both of their performances on the street."

"Well, I don't want to take up your whole afternoon. I'd better be going." Tom stated.

"I'll be right back," Olivia said. She went inside and returned with Sirius's leash in hand.

"Thanks, but I won't be needing that, I've got leashes and harnesses in my car," Tom stood and shook both Olivia's and Monty's hands. "Thank you for thinking of my fellow police officers and donating Sirius, provided he passes the temperament tests. We won't forget it. I'll give you a call in a few days and let you know how Sirius did on his evaluations."

"You're welcome," Olivia and Monty both replied. They went over to Sirius and said their goodbyes.

Mother came up behind them and nudged me.

I licked her face for what I thought might be the last time.

Jacob and I stood up. I liked the extra attention, but why did Olivia have tears on her face. Oh... I know I'm going out the gate just like Nova, Calypso, and Celeste did, and I'm not returning. If dogs could cry...

But, no I was ready, I knew I had a calling. I didn't know what it was until now. Although I had a hankering ever since I meet that police dog, Jacob.

Tom stepped down off the porch and started towards the gate. "Jacob, Sirius, Come! Let's go. Your first test, Sirius."

Olivia and Monty remained on the porch and watched.

The dogs followed with their tails wagging. When they reached the police cruiser, Tom opened the back door and they both hopped in. Tom shut the door, waved towards the house, and then drove off.

TEN

Once we left the bumpy farm dirt road, outside my window, trees flashed by. Tom lowered our windows enough for us to get a good snoot full. The pet place we passed by must have gotten a new shipment of treats. The air was heavenly. Then we sped up again, bound for out of town.

Seeing Jacob lay down for a nap, I joined him. An excellent idea! We both awoke when we stopped at a traffic light. Tall buildings loomed all around us now. They created giant shadows.

Tom rolled down his window and I smelled people scents. I whiffed, cologne, hairspray, deodorant, and sweat, mostly sweat, from workers in the middle of the street. They were surrounded by bright, little fences. I thought it was strange that some of those people who had funny hats on went into a hole in the pavement. But I was bewildered as to why some of them came back out of the ground with nothing to show for it. Truly those people could use a dog. ...and those little fences—they wouldn't keep anybody in or out.

I could smell various types of food odors, some made me salivate and others made me sneeze. Interesting, but it also made me hungry. The tall buildings were soon replaced with houses, houses with green grass surrounding them, not like the farm dirt.

We pulled up in front of one of them and Tom got out. He opened the door on the side where Jacob was.

"Come on boy, you've been riding all day. The kids are home from school and they're waiting to see you!" Jacob hopped out.

"Sirius, I'll be right back." He shut the door.

Tom came out shortly and we drove off then stopped at another house close-by.

"We're here!" Tom said, as he snapped a leash on my collar and motioned me out.

What's here? I thought. I saw the curtains move inside the front window. Two very small faces looked out. Tom rang the doorbell and I sat down and waited.

A tall man with friendly eyes opened the door. "Hey Tom, I thought you'd never get here. The kids are excited. This must be Sirius!"

"It is!" Tom exclaimed. "Sirius this is, Michael. ...and Michael meet Sirius."

Michael stooped down and stretched out his hand so I could get a good whiff of him.

My tail went into auto-wag.

Michael gently scratched me behind both ears.

Ah, he knows my spot, is that great or what?

"You're one handsome boy!" Michael stated.

I felt my tail speed up. I like him!

A woman came up behind Michael. Two children peeked out from behind her skirt.

"Pam," Michael said, "this is Sirius."

"Hey Sirius, welcome! My, what a beautiful dog."

She bent down and gave me a caress on the head.

My tail wagged some more and I licked her hand.

"He's so friendly, Michael, are you sure you want to turn him into a K-9 partner?" Pam giggled.

"Ha, ha," Michael answered. "Sirius come on in and meet Jenny and Jasper."

I took a step in and stopped so Jenny and Jasper could pet me.

Pam stepped aside and the kids slowly reached out to pet me. Jenny giggled when she felt my head and ears.

Jasper reached out and said, "Paw!"

He speaks my language. I raised my left paw and Jasper shook it.

"Good boy!" He said.

"Momma, Sirius is a south paw like me! Can he stay? Please... Please," He tugged on the bottom edge of her blouse.

"I hope so—we'll see," she answered. "Good to see you, Tom."

"You too, Pam."

"Let's all go out back and I'll fix us some snacks and drinks," Pam stated.

"Yea!" Jenny and Jasper shouted. "Hurray!"

I followed Jenny and Jasper towards the back porch door, stopping a few times to sniff my new surroundings.

Once in the backyard I scampered with my 'new little people'.

"Looks like the kids like their new playmate, I hope he can stay," Michael said.

"We'll find out tomorrow," Tom replied. "I'll be by tomorrow to pick Sirius up for his temperament test and basic obedience test. You're welcome to come along."

"I'm there. I've been waiting for an opening to come up in the K-9 unit for three years–ready to get started."

"Good, pick you two up at 6 a.m.!"

"We'll be ready," Michael affirmed.

"You'll have to watch Sirius tomorrow on close-circuit TV," Tom stated. "We don't want him to have any distractions while testing. Just policy, that's all."

"Sure, I understand," Michael answered.

"If Sirius passes he'll be in canine school for four months," Tom explained. "You'll be in separate handler training for two months and working with Sirius as a team for the remaining two months. Don't forget there's an additional 16 hours every month of team training.

"Can't wait! Four more months, huh?" Michael questioned.

"That's been our average, however, it's gone longer a few times. In the meantime, we've found that early placement of the dog with his future handler builds trust and confidence as a team."

"Yeah," Michael laughed, "I told the kids that a surprise would show up at the front door today. They've been staring practically non-stop out the front window all morning. I told them that the surprise might be here for just a little while. They said, 'Oh, Dad'—thought I was teasing. Then I said, 'Really... Your surprise could be here for only a few days.'

"Oh, and do you know what Jenny said, Tom?" She said, 'alright, a few days is better than nothing.'"

"Wow!" Tom replied. "My kid would've said, we don't want it if we can't keep it, Dad! Some great kids you're raising, Michael. Can I lend you mine for a few weeks?" Tom said laughing.

"Sure, what's two more," he grinned.

"I have returned," Pam stated. "I'll bet you two thought that I was never coming back." She sat down a huge tray laden with two different types of crescent sandwiches, coleslaw, potato salad, tea, and lemonade.

"You really did it up! Pam!" Tom exclaimed. "Thank you!"

"Yeah, Honey. This looks delish!" Michael stated.

Jenny and Jasper came running over with Sirius right behind.

"Starving!" Jasper shouted.

I saw the food and remembered that I hadn't eaten much this morning. I was too excited when I saw Tom pull up outside. My tongue was hanging out and dripping.

"Jasper, Jenny..." Pam instructed, "Before we eat run and get the dog bowls on the kitchen island. Jenny you do the water and Jasper you scoop the dog food like I showed you two this morning, okay?"

"They both answered in chorus, "Okay, Mommy!" They ran for the kitchen.

"Please, no running in the house," Pam shouted after them.

Jasper and Jenny returned and held the two dog bowls for Pam to inspect.

"Looks good! Please set them down in the corner of the patio."

Jenny and Jasper placed the bowls as instructed and stood by waiting for me to start eating.

I walked over and took one whiff. They have my food here, smells like my usual stuff.

I looked at the bowls, salivating.

"Why isn't he eating, Mommy?" Jasper asked.

Tom said, "Looks like he's been trained to wait. Let him know that it's okay, guys."

"Sirius, okay, boy, eat!" Jenny and Jasper chorused. They both pointed to the bowls.

"Step back a bit and let Sirius have some room," Michael said.

The kids sat down at the patio table and watched me.

I wagged my tail, chowed down and drank half the bowl of water, too!

"He was hungry and thirsty," Jenny said.

"Yeah! He was!" Jasper exclaimed.

"Well, big day tomorrow, everybody," Tom said. "I'd better be going. See you at 6, Michael."

"Thanks for everything, Tom," Michael said.

"Thanks, Tom," Pam said.

"Yea! Thanks Tom!" Jasper shouted.

"Thanks for the great dog!" Jenny exclaimed.

"My pleasure. Now take good care of Sirius, kids. I know that you will. He's a good dog!" Tom replied.

"He is!" Jenny answered.

"He's our best friend already!" Jasper exclaimed.

I liked my new, two little people. I didn't even care about the gummy bear stuck in my coat that I couldn't reach to eat.

ELEVEN

I slept well after crawling up on Jenny's bed in the middle of the night. Jenny put her arm around me and whispered, "Good dog." I did have a dream I remembered though. I think I recalled it because my paws must have jostled Jenny and I remember her saying in the darkness, "No kicking, Sirius."

The dream had me running full speed with Michael following behind me. My heart was pounding as we rounded a corner store inside a shopping mall. I saw a small child, a girl, by herself, with her feet off the floor, leaning over a railing, then I woke up. Even though I was moving at top speed my legs felt like lead. Everything that should have been wheezing by me, moved in a slow motion blur instead. I couldn't move fast enough no matter how hard I tried. I'm glad Jenny woke me up.

Light was just starting to filter through the curtains when the kids and I stirred. I followed the kids downstairs and Jasper let me out into the backyard after some convincing, because I smelled bacon cooking!

Once back inside, Jenny and Jasper prepared bowls of water and dog chow as I sat and watched.

Then they both shouted, "Okay, eat, Sirius!"

I chowed down in the corner by the kitchen table while everyone sat and ate that delicious bacon.

I walked over to Jasper's chair and sat down. A small piece of bacon floated by my nose, No... wait... it was in Jasper's small hand. I took it and chewed it thoroughly to get all of the flavor out before swallowing. I gave him a thank you nudge or maybe it was because I hoped another tasty morsel might find me— it was both.

"Jasper, new rule, no feeding the dog at the table." Pam stated. "Some food that we eat can cause problems in a dog."

"Sorry, Mommy," he replied.

Jenny gave Jasper a stern look. "Besides," she told Jasper, "my friend Monica said she never feeds her dog at the table because he will beg for food later."

"That's true, Jenny, very good!" Pam affirmed.

"Jenny, you're a smarty pants! That's what you are!" Jasper exclaimed.

"Uh-hem... we also have the no arguing agreement at the table," Pam stated.

"Okay... sorry, Jenny," Jasper stated with downcast eyes.

"What say we go to the pet store after we get dressed?" Pam asked. "You two can pick out some dog treats for Sirius?"

"Can we, Mommy? I'm going to get dressed, now. May I be excused?" Jasper questioned.

"You may," Pam replied. "... and you also, Jenny, if you are finished eating."

They headed for the stairs.

I followed behind them.

"Race you to the top!" Jenny challenged.

"Okay, count to three, then you follow me,"

Jasper said.

"Hey! No fair! We start together, Jasper Collins."

"Kids, please no running on the stairs," Pam declared.

"Our kids can be a handful sometimes, huh, Pam?" Michael asked.

"No question, but they are treasures," she said and smiled.

"They're gold just like their momma," Michael commented.

"Ah... now who is looking for more bacon at the table," she teased. "You sure have been quiet this morning, Michael. Is everything alright?"

"I'm a little nervous about Sirius passing his tests. The kids are going to be heart-broken if Sirius can't stay."

"He'll be fine, Corporal Collins," She leaned over and gave him a kiss.

"You're one of the first to call me corporal, sounds weird."

"Has a nice ring to it, Honey." She looked out the front window. "Tom just pulled up."

"Thanks," he replied. He kissed her on the cheek.

"Sirius, here!" he called up the stairs.

I hurried down the steps and sat as Michael fastened the leash to my collar.

"Bye, kids, see you, tonight!" Michael shouted upstairs.

"Bye, Daddy," they replied adding, "Bye, Sirius."

We headed out the door, both of us anticipating new horizons.

TWELVE

Michael opened the back door of the cruiser and I hopped in. Tom reached back from the front seat through the mesh cage screen opening and gave me a pat on the head. Michael climbed in the front seat.

"Ready, Michael?" Tom asked.

"I am. What part do I play in the temperament testing?"

"None. I strictly want you to be an observer, today. There'll be a handler involved, some others that'll be role players, we call decoys, and an evaluator, me."

"Where are we headed first?" Michael quizzed.

"The academy annex for some stability of character testing, detection testing, perseverance test retrieve and prey drive tests. Then we'll go in the field for water conflict and food conflict testing."

"Sounds pretty detailed, Tom."

"Well, there's a few more tests in the field, handler/object conflict test, a hunt drive test, an on-line search test, and a few more."

"Is that where the dog uses a search engine to apprehend a suspect?" Michael laughs.

"Funny..." Tom chuckled. "Nah, it's an on the leash search."

"I figured as much, just kidding."

"Keep that sense of humor, "Tom answered. "I

was on the street in K-9 for twelve years and without a sense of humor, I probably would have lost my mojo a long time ago. Tough job, but rewarding. You're always in the thick of things that's for sure."

I raised my nose and sniffed the air. I detected paw sweat as we rolled into a parking lot, probably mine. That raised my anxiety level a step. I was still confident and unafraid though.

Three police officers came out to greet us. They had cloth badges and name tags sewn onto their blue coveralls. They also had an already familiar K-9 patch like Jacob had on his vest. Tom and Michael stepped out of the car to chat.

Through the cracked car window I heard Tom introduce all three to Michael as Jensen, Miller, and Garcia. They were K-9 training handlers, two men and a woman.

Tom opened the back car door and snapped on my leash.

Finally, I thought. I was super ready to get out of the SUV.

"This is Sirius, guys!" Tom stated as I exited the backseat. "He'll be assigned to Michael after training."

Jensen and Garcia gave me a good look-over and patted me on the head. I tail-wagged and I raised my head slightly to acknowledge their pats.

"Huh…" Officer Miller said, as he looked me in the eye, his upper lip curled in disdain.

"Tom," Miller said, "can't you bring us a green dog that has potential? This dog looks like another washout if you ask me. He looks a bit small, too."

I met Miller's gaze and suppressed a growl. After all, I didn't want to fail the stable character part of testing. I wondered if Miller was that judgmental and mean or was this part of the test.

"He meets department criteria as far as physical attributes are concerned." Tom stated. "The testing will provide the data to determine his candidacy for the K-9 program. I'm of the opinion in my twelve years as a K-9 handler that Sirius has the potential to be a dual-purpose dog, as well."

So, Miller's belittling was real, I concluded. Well I've dealt with a bear. How bad could he be?

"Yes, Sir," was all Miller replied back to Tom.

"Garcia, you'll be the handler for testing."

She took my leash and all of us except Michael proceeded inside the side entrance to a gym area. Michael was headed to another part of the building to watch us on close-circuit TV.

I still sensed that Michael was around although I didn't see him nearby.

My handler, Garcia, walked me through another door into a busy large office. We walked around as I watched people scurry from place to place.

It seemed as if everyone wanted to greet me in a different manner. Some just stood and stared at me, not saying a word, but making sure they had good eye contact with me.

One even stood in front on me blocking my path, then they popped open a large umbrella in my face which initially startled me, but I held fast. It was no different than one of those roosters in the barnyard up in my muzzle and flapping its wings. I made sure that everyone got a good tail wag.

Tom lagged behind us with a handheld square in one hand and a stick in the other. I wondered if he would let me have the stick when he was done.

Garcia and I ran back out the exit door, to the gym ...and lo and behold there was a bowl of some good-looking dog chow and a new interesting squeak toy sitting next to it. She unsnapped my leash, then picked up the toy, squeaked it, and tossed it across the gym. She didn't utter a word though.

I paused for a second and eyed the food, trying to determine in my little brain what was important to her. Not the food.... Nah... ...the toy, she must want her toy back, and I wanted to check it out for myself, too.

I made a run for it. After I snatched it up, I gave it a few good quality test squeaks, then I returned it to her. Well, not exactly. I laid down in front of her and continued to squeak it. That is until she held out her hand again without saying a word. I knew what that meant. I placed the duck in her palm.

I heard Tom standing nearby say, "He's aced those two tests I'd say."

"He sure did," Garcia agreed. "Good, boy, Sirius!" She gave me a gentle pat."

I was beginning to like her a lot. Somehow, I couldn't put a paw on it, but she reminded me a little of Mother. I wondered if Rose Garcia was a hero, too, like her.

Officer Miller entered the gym and picked up the duck, squeaked it a few times, then waved it in front of my nose, but he didn't give it to me. Instead he rolled out a huge tractor tire out of a utility closet, pushed it over on its side and let it wobble until it lay flat on the gym floor. Then he placed the new squeak toy inside of it out of sight. I suspected that he probably enjoyed this part because he smirked at me after he placed the duck in it.

"Sirius, fetch! Get the duck, Sirius!" Garcia pointed towards the tire.

I'll show that Officer Miller that he was wrong. I ran to the tire and sniffed around the edges till I located where the duck was in the tire. I frantically scratched and bit at the spot to no avail. I've got to come up with a new plan... think, Sirius, think...

Then, it dawned on me. The tire was too heavy to move. This was a bonus-sized tractor tire. I had watched Monty and another farmhand one time try to flip one upright, and it took the two of them.

I stepped back, then took a flying leap up to the tire's top edge and managed to straddle the tire's side. My hind legs hung over the tire's outer edge, but I could see the duck, so I leaned forward and plopped down inside. I grabbed the duck and gave it a good squeak.

Officer Miller laughed and said, "Well, I told you so. That stupid dog is stuck inside the tire. No dog ever leaped inside the tire on a perseverance test and got back out. This should be fun to watch!" He laughed some more.

I heard that. Everything echoed throughout the gym. I hunched down on my hind legs and leaped upward. I caught a glimpse of freedom above the tires upper edge, but I didn't quite leap high enough to gain the tire's sidewall.

"Ha, ha! Look at that! I saw his head!" Miller exclaimed. "This is funny!"

Officer Garcia watched alongside Tom, who I had glimpsed. Tom still had his hands on his hips.

Okay... I said to myself. Remember way back, at least in dog years, your early days... you're a climber... Yeah, I am. Besides I won't let Mother down or Michael or my new siblings, Jenny and Jasper or my foster mom, Pam, down.

With the duck secured in my mouth, I tensed every muscle in my body and reared back on my hunches like a coiled spring and sprang upward.

It seemed like slow motion. I caught another glimpse outside of the tire, then my front paws touched the sidewall's outer edge. I struggled forward managing to rest on the tire's edge, halfway in and halfway out. I lowered by head and wiggled forward some more. Then, I was free, once again outside the tire and on the gym floor. I could lick that floor!

Actually, I could because Miller had dumped water on it, but I managed not to slip in it. I ran to Garcia and dropped the duck at her feet to applause from everyone, everyone except Officer Miller.

"You're right, Miller," Tom said. "No dog has ever done that before. Amazing, huh?"

Miller grumbled something and left the gym.

"Okay... well..." Tom chuckled. "He also passed the slick gym floor test. Time to move this party to the outside field areas."

THIRTEEN

It was good to be outside, however it wasn't long before I caught a familiar whiff just before we entered a red brick building. Olivia had taken me to a shooting range and I associated the gunpowder smell with a lot of noise. It just wasn't as loud as when that bear roared in my ear just before he swatted me to another galaxy.

Tom paused then entered one of a dozen booths. I liked to call them corrals. They reminded me of barn stalls in a funny kind of way.

Garcia and I walked down the hallway that lead to the booth where Tom was.

Tom removed his Smith & Wesson M&P 9 from a gun carrying case, inserted a magazine and closed the action. He leveled it at a paper target downrange. "Garcia, range is hot. Commence firing on your command."

Garcia said, "Commence firing, three rapid rounds."

We moved past Tom's booth as I glanced at Tom in his shooter stance, but I continued to follow Garcia's lead forward.

My ear pricked up as the rounds went off behind me. We turned and approached where Tom was again and stopped.

"Commence firing, eight rounds at random

intervals," Garcia commanded.

I held a steadfast gaze on Tom while he fired off the rounds. I managed to not even twitch my ears this time.

Tom made his gun safe and said, "Range is cold." He finished putting it in the gun case and rejoined us. "Well, how'd he do?" he asked.

"Passed with flying colors. ...probably could land a 747 next to him and he wouldn't shy away. The only thing was that he flinched his ears on the first round of shots."

I keenly watched Tom scratch his little stick on the square that he carried around.

"Rock steady, Sirius... " Tom commented. He gave me a head rub and said, "Good boy, let's move back outside to the obstacle course."

Outside, we approached a tunnel object I had never seen before. It had small cubes and spheres connected by pipes and didn't look big enough for me to turn around in. Whoever designed it I figured, had a lot of time on their hands, or they needed to use up all of their surplus plastic things. I sat and scratched my side with my hind paw.

Garcia and I walked to the closest pipe entrance, then she unsnapped the leash from my collar.

"Sirius, search... go and find...go!" She stooped down and pointed to the tube entrance.

I looked at her, then redirected by attention to the dark tunnel. I hoped she hadn't seen it in my eyes my 'have you lost your mind look?' that I reserve for special occasions.

I lowered my head and body to fit in the tube,

crawl-walking into the blackness, not knowing what I'd find.

I moved forward through several different sized spaces none of which I could turn around in. I smelled latex rubber ahead. That might mean one thing... a squeaker toy—at least I hoped so. Something small streaked by me in the dark, coming from the opposite direction. I couldn't identify its scent and I didn't bother to stop it. I hoped that I made the right decision.

I found the squeaker toy and snatched it up. It was that quacky duck again. I crept forward.

I'd been cured of any claustrophobia I had when I was a pup. One night I crawled into a chicken coop and the hen house's air became filled with feathers and squawking birds.

I couldn't fathom what the fuss was all about. I didn't look like a coyote. I couldn't turn around in there either so I laid down, closed by eyes, and tried to cover my nose with my front paws to keep the feathers out.

Eventually all of the chickens hit the exit. They left me on the floor covered in feathers. Monty rushed out of the house to see what all the fuss was about. He opened the roof hatch and found me. I had to endure being called a chick pea for a few days, but that wasn't so bad considering all of the ruckus I had caused.

I saw a glimmer of light ahead. The pipe was becoming even smaller as I moved forward. I crawled on my belly still clutching the duck until I reached the end and crawled out.

Standing up straight felt good.

"Good boy, Sirius..." Garcia praised, "...and you have the duck, too! Excellent!" She reached into her vest pocket and pulled out a dog biscuit for me, while Tom sat down a bowl of water.

After a brief rest, Garcia hooked the leash back up and we took a brief walk to the bottom of a steep grassy hill.

I watched as a new officer approached us with a small box. Garcia held my leash as I watched the new officer reach into the box and pullout a piece of a metal pipe. I think he wanted to play, because he threw the pipe up the hill so far that I couldn't even see it in the high grass.

I wanted to go check out the shiny new stick. I pulled at the leash. Garcia unsnapped it and I was off running. I could feel my hip muscles tighten as I went up the steep incline. When I thought I was close to where the thing had landed, I put my nose to the ground and tuned my keen olfactory sense to the task.

I swept the area and I was starting to get discouraged when I detected an uncommon smell in the grass. It was a metallic scent and that new officer's scent. He should have used gloves if he didn't want me to find it. Smart-ass dog was my next random thought... My nose touched metal. I pawed the pipe and picked it up in my mouth. Whew... hard... I would prefer a softer stick. I placed it back in the grass. I hoped that new guy had something better to throw in that box of his.

Garcia called me back to her side and she refastened the leash to my collar.

The officer with the box reached back inside it and pulled something else out. I couldn't tell what it was. We were too far away from him and his box.

Darned if he didn't throw the new thing way up the hill again. I suspected that his second-choice career must've have been to try out for Major League Baseball.

Garcia released me again after I pulled forward to see what might be up the hill this time.

I headed back uphill at full speed minus a few miles-per-hour for the incline.

With my nose planted to the ground I searched. I sensed a familiar smell nearby-wood.

No fooling this nose! I found it! I flipped it a couple of times with my left paw and satisfied myself that it was ok to pick up, I snatched it up. Softer... but, still not as a good as a squeaker or a knotted rope or a lot of other favorite toys of mine.

I dropped it when I heard Garcia summon me and streaked back down the hill. Once again she hooked me to the leash. I sat down and watched the new guy reached into the mysterious box.

What would he come up with next? I hoped that it I would be a duck. I think I had a thing for ducks due to my chicken encounters.

He reached into that box and pulled out something else. Of course, I thought... toss it way up that hill again... I'll find it—he did.

I yanked on my restraint and Garcia released me. As I was running up the hill another thought occurred to me. This was fun! Was I supposed to be having fun during K-9 testing and was I doing what was expected of me? Had I passed all of the tests so far?

With my nose brushing through the grass I now detected plastic.

It took me a little longer to locate what was thrown this time, however I found it alright.

Again, I rolled it over, sniffing it end to end. I picked it up and decided it was a compromise in hardness between that hard metal stick and the block of wood.

I lifted it skyward and with a head jerk, I managed to toss it a few feet... then I pounced on it. I heard Officer Garcia laugh down below, so I repeated my hunt and grab technique for effect.

She called me back to her side.

I watched Tom play with his stick and the square that he held it to.

Maybe... Tom would give me his stick when he's finished playing with it. It must've been a fun stick because he never lets go of it. I wanted it.

Something ate at me though as we took a short break. Through all these tests, there were few commands given. I had to use my instincts for most of the tasks. I wondered how Tom had rated me so far. I only had a 'good boy' to go by.

I do know one thing, they were testing my collective aptitude. I wondered what was next. I hoped not to fail. I wanted to make Mother proud. I knew Michael would be disappointed if I failed the selection test. I also didn't want to have to leave my new family and go back to the farm with my head down. I wanted to succeed for me, too.

Garcia led me over the hill and down to a small

pond. Garcia removed a nice red rubber ball from her vest pocket.

I wondered if she had any treats in there, too. No one was handing very many out so far today. That was another reason to worry.

With me still on the leash, she teased me with the ball, letting me almost have it, then taking it back. My interest was piqued.

She threw it across the small pond and it landed a few feet from the water's edge on the other side.

She released me and I headed full speed around the water's edge. That ball would be mine. I was thirsty, but this was no time to catch a drink. I needed to get to that ball before something or someone else did.

I snatched the treasure up and ran back to Garcia. It was my turn to tease her. Several times she tried to grab the ball from my mouth, but as soon as I put it within her reach, I backed off a few steps. I repeated the process a few times before dropping it at her feet. I hoped I hadn't errored. They had to know that all dogs love to play. I wasn't any different.

Tom started scratching his stick again on the little box he held.

We took a walk to a nearby overgrown field. The grass was higher than my ears. Garcia pulled out something else from another pocket in her vest. It looked to be a ball wrapped in a piece of cloth.

She lowered it down in front of my nose. I wasn't sure if I should bite it or sniff it until she solved it for me.

"Sirius, sniff, boy!

I took several good whiffs and retained the scent in my olfactory repertoire for later recall.

"Fetch!" she commanded, then she tossed it far into the tall grass.

This time the leash stayed on and I lead her into the grass jungle.

With my head down I headed to the general vicinity of the wrapped ball. I sweep the area and found the target rather quickly I thought.

That was confirmed when she said, "Excellent job, Sirius!" She reached into one of her fatigue pockets and pulled out a small treat which she gave to me.

I signaled my delight with a few wags.

She led us out of the grass and we followed a path to a warehouse looking building.

Another woman dressed as a civilian was standing outside the building's roll up door. She opened it, and Garcia and I proceeded inside.

It was semi-dark inside, lit only by the daylight pouring in from the open entrance. We approached a van and Garcia opened the front driver's door. She pointed inside and said, "Search, Sirius, find!"

I glanced up at her, wondering when she would produce a clue as to what to search for, but she didn't.

"Search, Sirius", she repeated and gave my leash a tug forward toward the van's step. She pointed inside.

I'll look, and maybe it will be something obvious she wants me to find or not. So I climbed into the cab and began my sniff.

Huh... nothing out of the ordinary in the front cab anywhere.

Garcia opened the van's slider and stuck her head in. "Sirius," she called. I made my way between the two front seats and into the back portion of the van.

"Search, Sirius!" she commanded.

I continued my sniff, climbing over some boxes to some shelves in the rear of the van. When my nose hit the third shelf up I stopped. I let out a low bark and gave a few wags to alert Garcia that there was a scent I recognized, the same odor I had detected in the grasses.

Garcia climbed into the van and reached into the container on the third shelf I had pointed to. She pulled out another cloth wrapped ball.

Yep, that was it alright. It looked and smelled like the same item I helped find before.

She reached into her pants pocket and produced another delectable treat which I accepted with all due haste.

"You are a good dog, Sirius" She gave me a nice pat on the head and a scratch behind the ears.

Those hide and seek games were my favorites so far today and I got more treats as we went along. We walked over to some metal stairs that went upward, disappearing into the dark on the floor above. I wondered if we were going up there.

FOURTEEN

With leash in hand, Garcia and I ascended the stairs until we reached the darkness. She clicked on a flashlight.

That helped me get my bearings a bit easier. I could see that everything, everyone had ever discarded was up here. Old tires, boxes, furniture, tins, parts to who knows what, a few stuffed toy animals and no other living things except me and Garcia. I did detect the faint scent of another dog having been here a day or so ago.

There were additional hazards, too like slick oil spots on the floor.

Tom was with us, but he always followed us at a distance carrying his rectangle and stick at the ready.

We walked around a bit while Garcia flashed her light beam around. She pulled a handkerchief out of one of her vest pockets and waved it in front of my nose.

I placed my snout on the cloth and took several deep breaths.

It smelled like... like... the shooting range-same smell-strange, I thought...

Then Garcia said, "Sirius, search! Search, boy!"

I lead her around with my nose down while she pointed the light at the area I was scanning.

I tugged hard at the leash when I detected a strong gunpowder scent.

It was a long trace through several cluttered aisles. It seemed longer in the dark surrounding us. But the scent grew as I went. I nosed an old box on a small table. I sat and gave Garcia a little woof.

She opened the box and pulled out a handgun. "Good dog, Sirius. You found the suspects weapon he hid."

My confidence was growing with every success. I knew that she was joshing about the suspect. If there really was a suspect I would have found him, too!

We headed back downstairs.

Tom, who stood with us, continued playing with his favorite stick while Garcia placed a secure muzzle on me.

We headed outside towards a different area on the training grounds.

Tom told Garcia to walk to the first designated holding decoy area and stand-by.

Something was amiss. I couldn't put my paw on it, but my neck hackles stood up. Garcia held my leash taught. Tom stood back about ten yards while Garcia and I stood watching and waiting, for what I didn't know.

A door swung open from a small hut in front of us and a dark clothed figure leapt out of it. The figure appeared smaller than it was because of the distance between us. He screamed a lot of words towards our direction, none of which I recognized from my past. His screeching carried full force on the wind that gusted in our direction.

The dark-clad figure pointed a finger at us and started throwing punches in the air, as if he thought he could reach us. But then... he stopped. He held one fist out straight, directly at us, except he now held something in his clenched hand.

I watched as he turned and ran, losing sight of him behind the hut.

I tugged at my restraint never once taking my eyes off the threat. Garcia gave me a little slack and we moved forward, closing half the distance to the man.

I heard Tom shout behind us, "Garcia, release Sirius!"

She unsnapped the lease.

I followed his scent nose down. I had a good whiff of him thanks to the downward wind. The door to the hut remained open. I found no one else inside.

The scent lead from the back of the shed, over a crest of a hill to a large tree. I moved around the tree trunk trying to find pick up the trail and found the scent oddly moving up the tree trunk.

I looked way up into the tree's foliage. Success... there he was, up there glaring at me! I jumped upward on the tree and let out a succession of intense barks.

I heard the man cuss and say, "Stupid dog"!

Garcia heard me and came running. "Good dog, Sirius you found the bad guy! Good boy!" She snapped on my leash and patted my head.

Tom was right behind Garcia and shouted up at the man, "Good decoy, Miller!"

If I had known it was Miller, I might have tried to climb the tree after him.

"Okay, Garcia," Tom said. "Let proceed to the runaway test, follow me."

We approached a ground marker in an area that looked like a developer had put in streets, but hadn't built any houses yet. There were a couple of vehicles parked on the vacant streets. We paused and sat, waiting and watching for what I didn't know. I was sure of one thing now, that police work was full of surprises both good and bad.

Just as the pace of things seemed to slow down a car door popped open and a man stepped out. He appeared larger when he turned toward us and pointed at us. He began to rant and rave while still pointing at us. I wasn't sure at this distance whether he held anything in his hand or not. A few seconds later he turned and ran away from us.

"Garcia, release him," Tom stated.

When I heard the unsnapping of the leash, I made a fast run for the decoy.

He continued to run, but I was closing in on him fast. He started yelling at me as I got closer.

When I was within a foot of him, I leaped forward, planting both front paws in the middle of his back. He went to the ground in a cloud of dust.

He had a metal pipe in his right hand that he swung towards me, except I stopped him halfway with muzzle strike to his right arm.

He started to get back up still clutching the pipe.

I struck him full force in the chest putting him down hard.

I let out a barrage of barks in a high volume that

surprised even me. That's when Garcia and Tom showed up.

"Good work, Sirius you got the bad guy!" She snapped the leash back on.

The decoy got back up.

I eyed him keenly to see if he was going to make any threatening move towards us. He didn't and started to walk off. He turned back towards us though and said, "That was the fastest I've ever been caught. What a hit, too!" He continued to walk away and waved both hands in the air as he left.

Garcia and Tom laughed and I felt like I had done well—only Tom knew that however.

Tom tapped his stick on the rectangle thing for a few minutes while I sat.

"Alright, on to the courage test, test three," Tom announced.

With my muzzle still on we headed out. Tom took the lead. I walked along on the leash with Garcia.

We approached another ground marker.

"Hold up at the marker," Tom said.

Garcia whispered to me, "We knew that, didn't we, Sirius?"

I gave her a tail wag acknowledgement.

There were a few metal storage building scattered around, but nothing else of interest until somebody ran out from behind one of them. They started yelling and held up one hand with only one finger extended. He pointed at us with the other hand while continuing to yell at us.

I recognized that voice. It was Miller…

I tugged at the leash. I needed to protect my new

pack and subdue the attacker.

"Garcia, release your dog," Tom told her.

She freed me again without a command. I sped across the open terrain straight for the threat. When I was about halfway there the decoy charged towards me throwing fist-pumps in the air and hollering at me.

I continued my pursuit, even managing to speed up a little more. When I had almost reached the man he started throwing leaves and grass at me.

I hit him with a full muzzle strike at chest height and he reeled backward, but he didn't go down. I struck him again in the chest before he could regain his balance. He went down this time.

He wasn't one to give up either. He started to get up.

I was determined to keep him subdued on the ground. I walloped him again as soon as he got on his feet.

Garcia and Tom showed up and Garcia refastened my restraint on me." Good boy, you are a warrior, Sirius," she remarked.

I didn't quite understand what a warrior was, except if what I just did would make me one, I definitely wanted to pursue it.

"Next, handler protection," Tom stated. "Right this way."

Tom started off towards a row of old brick buildings in the distance and Garcia and I trailed behind.

As we walked I started to feel down about how I was fairing through all of the tests. What if I just failed one? Would I still be a candidate for K-9 training? I knew there would be a lot of trials by fire if I did become a K-9 officer. So right here and now, I resolved to never get too low or too high. That would be my mindset. I had been down that road before, like the high, when I thwarted the bear attack, and the low, trying to recover from the bear's forceful smack-down on me.

...Always the next play I thought, that's what mattered. The last play was over and done.

I was in a new state of mind by the time my self-talk had ended.

Tom said, "Remember, Garcia keep Sirius on the leash and walk him on your left side, away from the buildings. Walk him down to the end of the last building. You know the rest of the drill.

"Got it, Tom," she answered.

We started off at a leisurely pace with me never knowing what came next. We were approaching the end of the second building when someone sprung out from the corner. He stated yelling and pumping his fists toward Garcia.

Garcia dropped the leash without a command.

I growled and leaped for the attacker.

I hit him with a muzzle strike using all my might. He reeled backward, recovered and came at me with a stick. I struck his right arm welding the weapon, but he still walloped me squarely across my shoulders twice.

Now this was getting personal. I backed up a step and leapt for his chest and planted both front paws there, followed by my muzzled head. He went down with me on top of him.

Garcia said, "Sirius, heel,"

I backed off the attacker and sat.

Garcia snapped the leash back on me and we both stepped back. "

Good boy, Sirius!" She gave me a pet and a treat from her vest pocket.

"Well... decoy," Garcia asked laughing, "Are you getting up today?"

The trainer/handler decoy raised his head only and looked up at us. "Is it safe to get up now?" he asked. "Man... that dog can hit— impressive. That's what I call handler protection!"

Tom who was busy nearby scratching the rectangle with his stick let out a chuckle. "Safe to get up, Jensen, Sirius has stood down."

Jensen got up and brushed himself off.

"We're headed for the finish line, test 5," Tom stated. "Right this way."

Garcia and I followed Tom in another direction.

"Okay, cable bite test time," Tom announced. "Hook Sirius to the cable, Garcia, remove his muzzle, then take a walk out of sight."

Garcia bent down and whispered in my ear, "You know I'm only leaving you here because I have to. Don't worry... I'll be back for you!" She gave me a hug and unfastened my muzzle.

I was ready for whatever might come next. I watched as she walked out of sight.

I noticed that there was one other dog staked out to a cable a little distance away, and a horse grazing nearby, but I didn't let that distract me.

Just as I was starting to enjoy the fellowship of a few other animals, Officer Miller appeared from behind a stack of old wooden crates. He yelled at me and started doing Karate chops in the air, directed at me. Then he pulled out a gun from his pocket and shot it into the air a couple of times.

He brought an arm covered with a bite sleeve towards me, it was the one with the gun at the end of it. I latched on hard to his sleeve and shook it hard a few times. I managed to loosen his grip on the gun and he dropped it.

Miller managed to pick up a stick and gave me two slaps across my shoulders. They didn't call those sticks, flexible agitation sticks for nothing. I held a firm grip on his sleeve though out the blows.

Then, Miller slipped off the bite sleeve and stepped back out of reach of the tether I was on. I released the now empty sleeve, growled a warning and watched him to see what his next foul move might be.

Miller walked off and I was glad to see it.

I wagged my tail as Garcia walked back in sight and released me from the cable.

"Hey, Sirius, good boy." She gave me several gentle strokes behind my ears and a treat.

"How did he do?" Garcia asked Tom.

"I'm headed back to my office to prepare a full evaluation report. Should be ready for review first thing tomorrow. I'll send a c.c. copy to Corporal Collins, too."

"Yes, sir," Garcia replied."

"Sirius... " She said to me, as we headed back towards the parking lot "...we will find out how you did in the morning."

FIFTEEN

Garcia met up with Michael in the parking lot. "Did you catch all the action?" she asked while handing my leash over to his outstretched hand.

Michael wrinkled his forehead and asked, "How do you think Sirius did?"

"I don't really want to say either way," Garcia answered. "Tom's sending out his evaluation first thing tomorrow. You'll get a copy. ...and I don't want to get your hopes up. He's an honest evaluator though, no question."

"It's just that my kids are crazy about Sirius," Michael replied. "Pam and I are, too. They'd be brokenhearted if Sirius had to go back to the farm. I don't think they'd quite understand all of it, no matter how I tried to explain."

"Michael, I've got to run and pick up my kids from daycare. They'll charge me a fortune if I'm late picking them up. Listen, don't worry yourself. I have a good feeling about this one. I'd be disappointed if I didn't get to be Sirius's trainer/handler."

"Thanks, Rose. I appreciate the sentiment. Have a good evening."

"You too, Michael," she replied.

On the drive home the day's events caught up with me and I slept on the car ride home. I had a dream though—call it a nightmare maybe... I dreamt that I had to take all of the tests over and over again until I passed. During the dream, Tom never looked up, he just kept that stick of his planted on the rectangle in his hand. Maybe that's why I never passed any of the tests, he didn't see me perform.

I heard Michael's distant voice saying, "Wake up, Sirius were home." I was glad to escape from that dream.

"Sirius," Michael let out a laugh, "all four paws were moving while you were asleep. You must've been dreaming."

He cupped my head in his hands and gave me a double ear rub.

"Come on, buddy." Michael smiled and said, "Let's go inside. The kids are waiting. I see them peeking out from behind the curtains."

Jenny and Jasper must have some dog genes in them because they greeted me like they hadn't seen me in a month.

I don't profess to have any sense of the passage of time like all dogs. For instance, if you lived with me and went out for five minutes or five hours you'll still get the same greeting. Everyone likes to feel that they're missed when their gone, same goes for me. So I give, that is, us dogs give love, dog kisses, and butt wagging greetings when you return to us, regardless of the time away.

I went out back to play ball with the kids before dark while Michael and Pam sat on the patio. I overheard my name being mentioned a couple of times so I knew that Michael was telling Pam all about today.

We all watched a few shows including Animal Planet, my favorite, before hitting the hay early.

The next morning I woke up before Jenny and Jasper and headed downstairs to see if anybody else was stirring. I found Michael on the couch staring at a rectangle like Tom did yesterday, except Michael's rectangle was big enough to set on his lap.

I wagged and brushed against Michael's leg.

"Hey, Sirius, you're up early. You probably couldn't sleep either, huh? No email yet from Tom, what say we go fix everybody some breakfast and get you some chow, too."

I followed Michael to the kitchen and sat while he banged around the cupboards.

He sat my filled-food bowl down then placed a fresh water bowl next to it. I chowed down.

Pam came into the kitchen. I paused my eating and gave her a wag.

"You're such a good boy, Sirius," Pam commented. She gave me a pet.

"You too, Michael—making breakfast and all," Pam kissed him on the cheek and patted his shoulder.

"Hear from Tom yet?" Pam asked.

"Not as of five minutes ago. I checked four times already. I'll keep checking, you don't have to worry about that," he replied.

"What time did you get up, anyway," she inquired.

"Around five or so. I tossed and turned for an hour, so I decided to get up and check the emails."

"Daddy! Pancakes!" Jasper shouted as he padded into the kitchen.

Jenny walked in behind Jasper, rubbing her eyes and yawning. "Pancakes... yum..." Jenny stated.

"You got it, guys. Pancakes coming up! Have a seat at the table and I'll bring you two some juice."

Jasper petted me and Jenny gave me a hug. I am one lucky dog!

After breakfast, Pam, Jasper, and Jenny cleaned up while I followed Michael to fetch his rectangle he left on an end table. He brought it to the kitchen table and sat down. I huddled down next to his chair. I had my pointed ears perked. I could sense the nervous vibes coming from Michael.

It was quiet at the table except for the occasionally rattle of a dish or a giggle by Jenny or Jasper as they finished cleaning up the breakfast dishes. I think Michael and I were both a little on edge because Michael's phone sang out a loud fog horn type of ring that made both of us jump.

Michael answered his cell phone and poked on the speaker icon. The next thing I heard was Tom.

"Michael, I wanted to notify you first. The report will be out in a few minutes, but I want to welcome both you and Sirius into the K-9 training program."

I looked up at Michael. His lower jaw had dropped. First time I've seen that look on him. If I could giggle I would have.

"Michael...? Are you there?" Tom asked.

"Yeah... I... was... just taking it all in—what you said. I'm ecstatic... Sirius's tail is wagging. I think he gets it."

Pam, Jenny, and Jasper gathered around us and Jenny whispered in my ear, "Sirius, you're going to be a police officer like my daddy." That's when my jaw dropped, too.

"Classes start Monday for you both at 7:00 a.m. sharp. Of course, you'll be in separate training for two months then train together for two months. Oh yeah... I forgot to mention the bad news."

"What's the bad news, Tom?" Michael asked.

"If all goes well with the initial training you and Sirius might have two more months in search and rescue training and bomb detection training."

"Seriously?" Michael inquired. "That would be fantastic—can't wait."

"Yeah, Sirius tests showed that he's a dual-purpose K-9 candidate, no question about it. Oh, and I know your track record, too, Michael. I think you would thrive in those other fields as well."

"Thanks for the compliment, Tom. We'll see you Monday."

"Looking forward to it," Tom acknowledged. "Check out the online report when you get the chance, Michael."

"Will do, thanks."

"See you, Michael. Bye."

My butt normally doesn't move with my tail wag except in a bout of joy. My back end was dancing. Jenny and Jasper stopped their cheering for us long enough to point to my hindquarters and say, "Look, Sirius is dancing." They both giggled.

"Congratulations my sweet... Corporal Michael!" Pam exclaimed.

"You too, Sirius." Pam reached down and gave

me a head rub.

"Yea... Daddy!" Jasper and Jenny chorused.

I watched Michael hug the kids.

He hugged Pam, too and told her, "Thank you, Honey!"

"Today's your last three to eleven shift for a while, Michael," Pam stated. "Hey... with your new regular schedule, for a while we'll have time to go shopping every weekend and out to dinner on every weekday like normal people." She laughed.

"Uh oh... I better call Tom back and tell him I've changed my mind." Michael grinned. "Nah... I'd enjoy the outings as much as you, maybe, just not every day. I'm all in, Babe."

SIXTEEN

The last patrol shift went by on the quiet side, Michael thought, as he drove back to the station. Just two domestics, a car thief apprehension, a motorist assist with a flat tire, and a breaking and entering after the fact. Since things were slow, I was lucky to get to hang around the B and E scene for a while and assist the evidence detectives in gathering crime scene evidence. That's always interesting stuff, he concluded.

"You can't leave yet, not without helping me eat these," Rick said to Michael back at the station. Officer Rick Ledger held up a bag of fresh donuts from the local Frosty Donuts store.

Three more officers walked in carrying coffees. The tallest of the three, Juan, said, "Yeah, let's have a donut fest, Michael, and you can tell us how you managed to connive your way into the elite K-9 core." He laughed and slapped Michael on the back and said. "Congrats, brother! Well done. You earned it!" He shook Michael's hand. The other two officers with Juan shook Michael's hand as well.

"Thanks," Michael said. "It's not like I won't be back on the streets, you know."

"Except you'll have a dog as a partner," Rick stated, "I'm jealous. All I ever got to ride with me was an elitist T. O." Rick said, pointing a finger at

Juan.

"Hey!" Juan said, "You're lucky I was your training officer or you would have washed out. Now look at you, you're the epitome of excellence, one of the department's finest!" He grinned.

"I'll vouch for that," Michael agreed. "Best apprehension/conviction record last month—come to think of it, the last three out of six months."

"Hey, cacklers, one of the officers that came in with Juan said, "What say we drink these brews before they get cold. I'm dressing out of these blues and I'll meet you gents in the break room in five flat."

When the donut-coffee party in the break room hit the ninety minute mark, Juan remarked, "Well, fellow scouts, it's been fun, but I gotta run."

"Yeah, and you're a poet and don't know it," Rick answered back. He was seated next to Juan and gave him a playful punch in the shoulder. "You just want to get home to the misses that's pining for you. "Ah!" Juan grinned. "That's right, go home and hug your pillow!" He teased.

"Alright, alright," Michael laughed. "Who spilled the beans about Rick being the lonely guy?"

The room erupted into fits of laughter.

"Now I really need to get home, guys," Rick stated. "My pillow probably does miss me. I have goose down pillows, you know?"

When the second round of laughter slowed, they said their goodnights and headed home.

SEVENTEEN

I heard Michael drive up so I peeked out the front curtains. Jenny saw my tail wagging and shouted, "Daddy's home! Yea!"

I stood by the front door behind Jasper and Jenny waiting for it to open. When it did, the kids wrapped themselves individually around each of Michael's legs so he couldn't take another step forward.

"How's my favorite anchors?" He teased. "Let me go so I can give you a super hug!"

They both released their hold and Michael stooped down and hugged them both together, "I missed you two!"

"We missed you, too, Daddy!" Jenny stated. "Sirius missed you, Daddy. Look he's sad." She pointed at me.

Jenny and Jasper both stepped aside allowing me room to move forward.

I gave Michael a nudge and a lick. Olivia had said once, back on the farm, that I had a licker license—must be true.

"...and how is Sirius?" Michael questioned. "He doesn't look sad now. His tails wagging and he has a toothy doggy smile."

Michael patted me on the head and gave me a head hug. The kids were right, I was glad to see him.

"He was sad earlier," Jenny restated.

"Yeah, he was," Jasper added. "He's okay, now."

"How about you two showing me the work you two did in school today?" Michael asked. "Where's Mommy at?"

"She's in the kitchen," Jenny replied.

"Come on," Jenny giggled, taking Michael's hand in hers. "I'll introduce you. That's one of the words I learned today."

"Wow, that's a big word," Michael commented.

"I learned about the duck-billed platypus," Jasper said.

"That's fantastic," Michael said as they all walked towards the kitchen. "You're going to have to tell me all about it."

"Hey, honey. Glad you're home safe!" Pam kissed him. "At least you have the weekend to relax a little before you start your academy class on Monday."

"This was the eighth day of shift three," Michael replied. "Glad to be off it for now. I love my job, but I was never too crazy about the rotating shift part— goes with the territory though."

"Sit, dinner will be ready in a half-hour," Pam said.

"Plenty of time to sit later, Honey, thanks," Michael replied.

"Come on, kids," Michael said, "let's go have a fun checkout of your schoolwork.

I padded up the stairs behind them, not wanting to miss the fun, either.

After a while I began to get sleepy. I didn't want to start yawning and let the kids think they were boring me, they weren't. I just needed a nap. The rigorous battery of tests had finally caught up with me. So, I found my duck, gave it a squeak and headed for a quiet corner downstairs.

When I woke up I didn't feel right. My stomach was turning and I felt like I was going to vomit. I headed for the back door and did a multi-nail tap on the glass sliding door, hoping to be let outside before I messed up my house.

"Okay, Sirius. Must be an emergency, huh, based on the extra tapping." Pam slid the door open, just in time.

I heaved a couple of times on the grass and kept my head down in case there was more. I started to shiver. I laid down.

Pam hurried out and placed a hand on my head. "Your shivering, boy" She felt my ears and touched my nose. "Warm, huh," she said. "Sirius, you're one sick dog. Stay here. I'll go get Michael, I think we need to visit the vet's."

Michael came outside with Pam and the kids and he repeated what Pam had done. "Sirius, buddy, we need to get you to the doc's."

"I'll call the vet's," Pam stated, "...and then get the kids in the car, Michael. You bring Sirius and a few large old towels for the back seat. Bring a blanket, too, Michael."

"Okay," Michael replied.

"Sirius, I'll be right back," Michael told him. "I need to get your leash, too."

I raised my head and managed to sit up.

Jenny and Jasper stood still close by. They were keeping a close watch on me.

"Is he going to be alright, Daddy?" Jenny asked.

"I hope so. We need to get him to the vets. Go with Mommy, please, Honey."

"Okay," Jenny answered. She turned to leave, but kept looking back at Sirius as she walked away.

"Poor, Sirius," Jasper said. He gave Sirius a light pet on the shoulders.

"You, too, Jasper," Michael said. "Please go with Mommy, and I'll bring Sirius to the car, okay?"

"Okay, Dad," he replied.

Michael found my leash along with towels and a blanket that he had tucked under one arm. We walked a slow walk to the car. I managed not to vomit again, but I felt as poorly as I ever had, except for one other time. That was the time after my bear encounter that sent me to the animal hospital.

I smelled the disinfectants and bandages as we approached the animal hospital's parking lot. I wasn't particularly fond of those smells either, based on my past experience.

Michael talked to some nice people at the big desk in the middle while Pam lead me and the kids over to a bunch of chairs and small couches, complete with little tables with magazines on them. I knew that they were trying to make like, this was a home living room, but they weren't fooling me. I knew the butt poke was coming soon and it was the worst mostly.

I laid down on the floor and tried not to make eye contact with any of the other dogs. I was just too ill to socialize right now. Maybe catch me on the way out of here, guys, I thought.

I raised up into a sitting position and produced a dry heave. I'll bet the doctor's assistant was glad about that, not to mention the other people in the room.

Michael felt my nose and ears again.

"Is he still running a temperature, Michael," Pam asked.

"Yeah... still feels pretty warm, poor Sirius." Michael stroked me lightly behind my ears.

A young girl in a doctor-like outfit came over to see us. She had the familiar rubber thing around her neck. I thought it looked like some kind of weird chew toy, except I didn't think they would appreciate me chewing on it. I didn't feel up to it anyway.

"Hi folks, my name is Tabby, hi Sirius," she said, and bent down to pet me.

So what seems to be going on with Sirius today?" She asked.

"He been vomiting and seems to be running a temperature," Pam answered.

"Yeah," Jenny added. "Can you make him better? Please... He's my big brother."

"Hey!" Jasper exclaimed. "I'm your big brother, remember?"

"You are both my big brothers!" Jenny declared.

The others in the waiting room smiled.

"Well..." Tabby answered. "Let me take Sirius in the back and examine him, okay?"

"All righty," Jenny answered.

I got up slowly and prodded along next to Tabby who had my leash. Michael followed. I think Tabby picked the examining room the furthest away. I thought we'd never get there.

Pam stayed back with kids, since the room we entered was tiny.

Michael lifted me up onto the slippery exam table. This is how a sacrificial lamb feels, probably. I had seen that scary image on TV. I need to quit watching TV so much, well except for Animal Planet.

I stood up for the all too unpopular temperature check. Tabby asked a few more questions on vaccinations, diet, and how long I had the symptoms. Then she said, the doctor will be right in. She turned and left.

"It's okay, boy. We're going to get you fixed up." Michael rubbed my head, neck, and back while we waited.

The vet came in and in a friendly tone of voice said, "Hi, I'm Doctor Fletcher. So, Sirius is not feeling his normal self today."

He gave me a couple of reassuring pets. Next he looked in my ears, then lifted my gums on both side of my muzzle. "Looks good, so far." He read through my chart and asked Michael a few more questions. One of them was about water. That made me thirsty. I hadn't wanted to drink anything all day.

"I believe he has a stomach virus based on everything I've seen and heard," Dr. Fletcher advised. "I'd like to keep him overnight and administer some electrolytes. He seems to be a little dehydrated and I'd like to keep a watch on him, just as a precaution. We have someone here monitoring our patients 24/7. We'll try some light foods as well, as soon as he's feeling a little better."

"Well, that's a relief," Michael replied. "I was worried that it might be something more serious... Okay."

Michael bent down and said to me, "Sirius, we are going to miss you tonight. We'll pick you up just as soon as we hear from Dr. Fletcher." He gave me a light hug.

I was going to miss them more, but I wasn't much use to anyone right now in my present condition. I sighed.

Michael and the doctor shook hands and I was escorted off to the back area. What a way to celebrate my new police dog recruit status, I thought. I worried that they might toss me out of the program if I didn't show up for Monday's first day of training.

EIGHTEEN

The day crew at the vet's went home and it became quieter except for the occasional bark from a homesick dog. An assistant who introduced herself as April, checked on me and the tube wrapped in a cloth on my front paw.

April was nice. She gave me a small amount of water to drink and a small bite to eat every once in a while. Other than that, I slept and had dreams of running with the kids in the backyard.

After daylight started to come through the small windows across from my kennel, I became restless. I was feeling much better and missed my family and my own bed.

April had left a short while ago and told me 'goodbye' before leaving and 'I hope you are feeling better and get to go home today.' She was a sweet girl. I could smell another dog's scent on her as soon as she had arrived for the overnight shift.

I watched as Dr. Fletcher came into the room and approached my kennel. I wagged my tail, hoping it would help punch my ticket out of here.

"Good morning, Officer Sirius," he said to me with a smile.

Now he was gaining points! That was the first time anyone had called me that. I liked the sound of it. I had heard others address Michael as officer also.

"How are you feeling today?" the doc asked as he opened my kennel door and conducted a brief exam of me.

Satisfied that I was feeling better, he removed the IV and I stepped out of the cage.

An assistant came over to talk to me and petted me while the doctor took my temperature, the not fun way.

"Sirius," the doc said, "you're going home this morning. Come on," he motioned for me to follow him to his office.

Once in his office, the doc said, "Let's call your kin."

I next thing I heard was Michael's voice—it was music to my perked ears. I was going home!

The rest of the weekend went uneventful, thank goodness! I rested and gradually resumed my normal diet.

As daylight peeked through a window once again, I awoke from my sleep when I heard Michael say, "Sirius time to wake up and get your breakfast. We need to head out soon or we'll be late for our first class."

I got up quietly, checked on the kids who were still asleep and hurried downstairs.

NINETEEN

On the way to training Michael put on some soothing music he called jazz. It seemed to take the edge off for me, too. Although it wasn't as good as hanging out the window, feeling the wind, and checking out the scents. I couldn't anyway, Michael hadn't brought my goggles this time.

Michael bought me the goggles for open window car rides just not in the patrol car. Guess it was unbecoming of a peace officer to be hanging out the police car window.

He also fitted me with a K-9 body-armor vest like the protective vest he wears. The vest didn't say police on it or have a badge on it either... maybe soon, I hoped.

We rolled into the training academy's parking lot and walked to the side of the building where the K-9 training entrance was. Garcia met us at the door and Michael handed my leash over to her. I gave her a wag and she returned the favor with a pet.

I was glad that it wasn't Miller. He gives me some bad vibes. I can't quite put my paw on it, but my dog's intuition flashes red whenever he's present. I need to get the negative thoughts out of my brain and concentrate my energies on learning as much as I can, no matter what comes.

I knew Michael would study hard, too, and I

didn't ever want to let him or the rest of my pack at home down.

The first week we worked on obedience. I was pretty good at following commands from the farm training Olivia had given me.

Michael also had worked with me a few times. He must have been impressed because I heard him say many times over, that's my dog, good boy, and you're awesome, whatever that is. He gave me a few behind the ear scratches on the 'awesome' so I figured that word meant, good stuff.

Week two we worked on agility. I liked the hurdles and the running between the cones. The stairs were easy until they removed a few of them, but I still managed the climb. After all I was a climber by nature, from my very beginning.

The warehouse was difficult to navigate with all kinds of boxes, poles, ropes, and other stuff strewn about. I was doing fine until I hit a large greasy spot on the floor. There was no way around it. I tried going through it at a fast walk. That didn't work! My back legs slipped, sending me on my butt. I made up my mind to try to finesse it the second time around. That worked better, only a little slip here and there. I managed it though.

Michael seemed to be doing alright, too. He had a few new books on the floor in the back seat. He would carry them into the house and only look at them late at night while everyone else was asleep. Sometimes if I heard Michael get up I would go lie next to him at the kitchen table. He would stare at the books and a new rectangle he got from training, then I would fall asleep. The next thing I knew, light was coming through the windows again and when I looked up, Michael was still staring at the books and rectangle.

On the second weekend after the beginning of K-9 school we packed up a picnic, and my family and I headed for an adventure at the state park nearby.

Michael remembered to bring my goggles so I got to hang ten out the back car door window. It was good fun except for the bug that flew up my snout. That caused me to have a sneezing fit that ended in the bug's first ejector seat ride.

Jenny and Jasper watched the bug shoot out my nose and hit the back of the seat where it stayed.

"Ugh, Sirius, gross!" Jenny shouted.

Even Jasper who was no stranger to bugs, worms, or even spiders, made a squashed-up face. All I knew however was that my nose felt better and I stopped sneezing.

"Mom, Sirius snooted up a bug on the back seat!" Jenny exclaimed.

"Is that what all that sneezing was about?" Pam laughed and reached back with a Kleenex in hand and snatched up the bug.

"Good job, Mom!" Jenny stated.

"Nice work, Mom!" Jasper added.

"Thanks, guys," Mom replied.

I went back to enjoying the breezes outside my window, hoping for no more wayward insects and kept a keen eye out for the park.

We hiked a trail by a stream staying on my leash due to state park rules. I didn't want to stray too far away from my pack anyway due to the fresh memory of my bear encounter. We picnicked by the stream and all was well until I smelled a bear.

I stiffened my tail and raised my nose upward sampling as much of the air as my lungs could hold—pine cones was all I could detect... no bear.

I turned in the direction towards the stream where my family was still busy eating. There was the scent again. There was a bear nearby. It was closer now.

I ran to Michael and bumped his arm nearly knocking his sandwich out of his hand.

"What's gotten into you, boy?" he asked, with a puzzled expression.

I barked once and whined. Then I turned towards the stream as if to point. Pointing wasn't my thing, but I had seen how it was done from an Irish setter I knew. The skill came in handy now.

Michael and I spotted a large black bear approaching the other side of the stream. He was getting bigger. He was headed towards us, but still on the opposite bank.

"Okay, guys," Michael advised, "let's have some fun and walk backwards towards the trail. Leave everything here."

Pam saw the bear, too now. "Jasper, Jenny, do as daddy say's."

"Ah... Mom, we didn't get dessert yet," Jasper complained.

"I know, Honey. I promise, we'll stop and get ice cream cones on the way home. Let's go."

They walked backward to the trail, all of them except me.

I saw the black bear getting closer, taking whiffs

of the air. The bear paused and fixed a long gaze directly at the picnic spread and me.

I heard Michael's voice arrive on a sudden wind gust. He was calling me. I retreated and caught up with my pack on the trail back to the car. There was one thing that was taught every day in my K-9 training, 'come when called.' I could see why now. It may have saved me today.

I'll bet that bear ate our desserts, but I got ice cream, a doggy ice cream on the way home. It was a fair trade.

TWENTY

There wasn't any hint of light coming through the windows when I heard Michael call my name from downstairs. I climbed out of my bed, did a butt in the air, front paw stretch and headed down the stairs. It must have been time to go back to training for Michael and I.

We ate breakfast together and headed out. Michael dropped me at the same entrance door where Garcia was waiting.

Rose Garcia was becoming my favorite trainer. She did most of my training. I liked the way she instructed me on what I was supposed to do. She would even demonstrate the technique she was trying to teach me if the need arose.

Once in a while we took field trips to the city. We were working on tracking through alleys on the outskirts of town, when I found a scent that eventually lead into a large cement pipe under a bridge. I looked inside and paused. All I could see was total darkness within.

It was one of Garcia's 'watch me, Sirius' moments, She dropped my leash and marched into the darkness. Once I saw that it was alright to move into unknown darkness, I was okay with anyplace that I had to go where I couldn't see. I learned to rely on my sense of smell and hearing. That kept me out of trouble.

We later worked on what Garcia called, apprehension, using a decoy with a bite suit. Capturing bad guys, I found was dangerous work. One of the decoys, Officer Miller, smacked me so hard with a flexible agitation stick on the head that I saw stars, but I held on to him.

Tom happened to be nearby and Miller got yelled at for that one. That put a big doggy grin on my face. Miller only reaffirmed my suspicion that he was really working for the bad guys or should have been.

I liked to search for evidence better than tracking the bad guys. There was always a variety of things to find. I likened all of this training to a game of hide and seek. I had plenty of practice playing the game with Jenny and Jasper around the house. It didn't take me long to find anything or anybody.

In the next several weeks we covered open area chases, building searches, and protecting my handler. Garcia didn't have to give me too many instructions for protecting her. Something took over in me when it came to protecting family and those that depended on me.

The last few weeks before graduation we went over everything we had covered before, along with a few new exercises.

Michael continued his late night studies at the kitchen table and I never missed a session. Well... I was there physically and in spirit, I just couldn't keep my eyes open, that's all.

One day, Michael and I sat face to face. He held my head in his hands and looked into my eyes.

"Sirius, tomorrow's a big day—graduation day! You'll officially be a certified police dog. What do you think of that, boy?" he asked.

I caught his excitement and stood up. My tail felt like it had hit its maximum wag. My tail had a mine of its own, like a mood meter on display.

Although, Michael didn't have a tail like me, I had a natural inclination to assess Michael's mood no matter what emotion he showed or tried to hide. We were in tune.

I'll always remember the day at the police academy when they pinned my badge on my vest. My vest now had the city police department patch and 'Police K-9' emblazoned on it in gold letters. Michael pinned on my badge and Tom swore me in. I raised my right paw for that. I looked up into the bleachers and Pam had a tear running down her cheek. Jenny and Jasper were waving and smiling. I love those guys!

Finally, Michael and I could finally work together as a team for the final two months of handler and canine training.

But the education wouldn't end there. I had heard Tom tell Michael, that there would be an 11-week course on explosive detection that followed.

Tom had designated me as a dual-purpose police dog. I'm not quite sure what all that means yet, but if I could serve and protect the community in more ways than one I was all in.

TWENTY-ONE

Pam had planned a party the night of graduation for Michael and me. A few of Michael's officer friends and their families came over. One of them was Officer Brett Carpenter and Jacob whom I had met a while back on a walk by a construction site with Olivia. Brett was Jacob's handler now that Tom was head of K-9 training and off the street.

Jacob and I ran with Jasper, Jenny, and four other kids in the backyard trying to pick up every ball in the yard before they did. I learned one thing though, you can only fit but so many different size balls at a time in your mouth.

I thought I was high-energy until I tried to keep up with all of the kids. It was lots of fun after all the hard work I had put in, except... whew... I was gonna need a good nap when the party's over.

Jacob took a breather every once in a while and sat down to watch us. Jacob was older than me and had been on patrol for a good five years. That was about half of a lifetime for a German shepherd.

The party ended as the sun was getting lower in the sky and I took that much needed nap with the kids. All of us were laid out in the middle of the living room with pillows from the couch and a throw. I do remember hearing Pam saying to Michael just before I nodded off, 'Ah, look at them napping together, how sweet is that.' I heard Michael say to Pam, ' Take a pic of them.' I woke up to what I felt was a short snooze, but the sunlight had faded away and the windows were dark.

We had supper together and I got a mighty meatball courtesy of my brother Jasper's drop. I don't know if it was on purpose or not, except I do know that it was mighty tasty.

Afterwards we piled into the living room and watched a movie about a dog who saves the boy who adopted him. I don't think Pam knew the ending when she rented it.

The mountain lion in the flick has a tussle with the dog who is defending his boy and saves his life. But the lion reappears late one night on the family's farm. The second meeting didn't go well for that poor, courageous dog.

Jenny, Jasper, and Pam cried. Michael snorted a few times and wiped his cheek with his sleeve before anyone saw. I let out a whine when the movie dog died and that got everybody back into a better frame of mind. They laughed. I didn't mind. I got a lot of ear scratches, pets, and a dog treat to boot.

Monday came all too fast. Michael and I headed back to the police academy for the beginning of our two-month team training.

All that extra late night studying that Michael did paid off, because when Michael took over from Garcia as my handler it went without a hiccup.

Michael and I went through a rehash of the previous two months training exercises together, as a team this time. I heard Tom say that as a newly formed team, we had concluded all of the exercises faster than any new team he had on record.

That got Michael and me into explosive detection early.

Michael said, I was gonna be a 'bomb dog'.

I began to learn to look for the components of bombs, not the bomb itself. A bomb could be hidden anywhere and take any form. But I found that the chemicals and substances smells were always present and would led to the explosive.

When I found chemicals in the families of explosives like, powders, commercial dynamite, TNT, water-gel explosives, or stuff like RDX used in C-4 or say, Semtex, I was instructed to sit close to it and not disturb it. I received a treat every time I found some of it whether it was a trace or a whole bunch. It was an easy way for me to score treats.

I made a game of it. There would be rows upon rows of cans and I would start down each row eagerly, wagging my tail as I went. I would do a snort, snort, sniff, snort, sniff, for each can until I found an explosive component. Then I would sit close to the can and wait for my treat. I would always get a 'good dog' as well! It was fun work.

I also learned to do searches on where the explosives originated from, too. Sometimes the search lead back to a particular house or car, or it sniffed back to some clothing and even to the hands of the bomber suspect.

I maxed out my rewards by finding every type of random chemicals and substances that they could stash in the various cans.

Next, the game moved to level two. Now I was

finding the stuff in suitcases, backpacks, boxes, and just about anything you could imagine. Sometimes it was just a small trace on a zipper or a handle or a flap, maybe... I found the bomb smells in buildings, vehicles, a stroller once, and even out in the open. It could be just about any ol' place. But I always earned my treat.

I was getting restless. I wanted to go on patrol with Michael and put all of these hard-earned instincts to use. I wanted to help rid my city of the bad apples.

I could sense that Michael was ready to hit the streets, too. He started this new habit of drumming his fingers on tables, countertops and such. I would look up at him when he would start drumming and he'd say, 'Sorry, Sirius,' and stop.

I think Pam was worried about how safe Michael and I would be on the K-9 team. I could sometimes smell trace amounts of her sweat when she woke up in the mornings.

Pam's worry started after a late night talk that Michael and Pam had. Pam asked Michael if K-9 teams answered all calls like Michael had done before. He said department policy set out the types of calls for K-9 teams. 'What type of calls, Michael?' I heard Pam ask. Michael replied, 'Let me get my manual—the list is long and specific.' He returned and Pam scanned the list in silence. She read:

Canine Deployments Shall Be Limited to the Following Situations:
Felony Crimes:
Burglary, not including trespass with non-violent secondary crime

Robbery, not including thefts that are accompanied by low level assaults

Homicide

Serious Assault

Kidnapping

Arson with threat of harm to people

Domestic Violence felony crimes

Sexual Assault

Drive by Shooting, not including unlawful discharge of a firearm.

Misdemeanor Crimes:

Domestic Violence Assault

Domestic Violence Order Violations that are subject to mandatory arrest—violations shall involve the subject's physical presence at the victim's location or a threat of harm.

Pam looked up from the page and didn't say anything for a few moments, then she said, "Well it's not like you haven't been on all of those types of calls before, right?" She inquired trying to erase a look of concern from her face.

Michael laid his hand on top of hers. His eyes met hers. "I'll do my best to be safe, Honey, don't you worry. Beside, I've got Sirius by my side now."

She smiled. They kissed, and I closed my eyes and went off to romp in doggy land.

TWENTY-TWO

I remember the last day of training. Michael and I received explosive detection certification cards that I saw Michael stash in his wallet. We still had to attend sixteen hours of team instruction every month, but that was small potatoes compared to what we had already gone through.

We got to leave early from the academy that day, Friday. Michael took me to a doggy park on the way home. It wasn't the first time that I had been to a dog park though. Somehow, Michael knew that I needed to unwind that day. He was good at reading my moods after all the time that we had spent together. I could sense his spirit as well.

The big dog section of the dog park had a few labs who were busy socializing with each other, a friendly setter, a big poodle, and another shepherd, a female.

I couldn't take my eyes off her. She seemed disinterested in me, however, only glancing my way twice.

The setter and I hung out together fetching balls that Michael and the setter's owner threw for us until the daylight started to fade. We headed home where Jenny and Jasper dished up some really good doggy treat ice cream for me.

The weekend flew by. We went to a local pet

warehouse store where Pam and Michael bought me a few new squeakers, a turkey and a new duck. I greeted any and all shoppers that paid me any attention and gathered quite a few behind the ear scratches and pets.

Next, we headed to a few other pet-friendly stores where I made a few more friends, then we stopped at a local park that sported a playground. I figured that this was the equal of a doggy park, except it was for kids. Pam, Michael, and I sat at a picnic table nearby and I kept a watch on the kids as they giggled on the play equipment. I loved to see them clown around and have fun.

It was a busy Saturday, so Sunday we rested in anticipation of Michael and I's first day on K-9 patrol on Monday. It would be the first day of the K-9 'alpha shift', four 12-hour shifts known as the day watch, 6 A.M. to 6 P.M. The night shift called the 'bravo shift', 6 P.M. to 6 A.M. would follow after a few days off in between.

TWENTY-THREE

During roll call, the briefing sergeant told Michael to report to the maintenance garage to pick up a new unit. I wasn't sure if 'unit' meant me or something else. It was an ear-lowering ride to the maintenance garage.

Were we ever going to get on the street together? I wondered... What the 'unit' turned out to be was a new police-packaged Ford Explorer that had more room than Michael's old cruiser which made it better for both of us.

I had my own safe separate place in the back that allowed me a little more space to stretch out if I wanted to. We finished moving our equipment from the old unit to the new, then took a required test ride. Michael checked out the radio, a lot of flashing lights and a siren that had a lot of additional sounds, more than the old cruiser had. He went through the whole SUV and we ended up taking the new unit back to the maintenance garage for a problem with the brake lights.

We sat in a waiting area while the shop mechanics had at it. Michael read a police magazine while I laid at his feet. It seemed like we had been there a long time, except I had no idea how to track time. All I had to measure by was my own bio-rhythms and the sun tracking across the sky during the day. At night, I used the temperature drop that came with sundown to track time.

When the sun was right above us, a mechanic brought the key fob out to Michael. He had Michael autograph one of those rectangles, then we hit the road. I heard Michael tell dispatch that we were 10-8 and I heard the dispatcher say, "I copy that, K9-7, in-service, at thirteen hundred hours."

Michael had taught me our call sign, K9-7, so if I heard it in the cruiser, I would know that I might be needed soon. My ears perked up whenever I heard it and it put me into a service-ready mode.

Michael had also told me that the city police radio communications center, like many police departments, had changed to plain English from algebra-like 10 codes and the like. I could better understand the calls over the radio that way.

Also, the many different police departments across the country could better understand each other with a common language in joint department emergencies like September 11 and Hurricane Katrina.

Although a few of the old common codes were still used and a few more were slipped in. It was no problem though, because every officer had a copy of the old radio codes and most knew them by heart.

Michael tried also to relate to me that my friend, Jacob, the longest tenured police dog was K9-1. Michael kept repeating, Jacob... K9-1, and he would make a funny expression each time he said it. So, I kept tilting by head from one side to the other, pretending not to understand him just so Michael would make the funny face again. I guess it was my dog humor at work.

No calls came our way right away so I just watched the city pass by the windows. We did go as a back up to a domestic dispute with a firearm, but we were the fourth unit to arrive so we cleared the scene and patrolled some more.

Just as soon as I had laid down for a bit, I heard K9-7 come over the radio.

Michael replied, "K9-7."

"K9-7, officers require assistance for a robbery suspect, 10-32, shots fired, 1414 West Dunaway Street. Officers on the scene advise, that you pull into the back alley only, behind the address for a meet."

Michael replied, "10-4, en route."

Michael flipped on the siren and I saw the blue and red flashes reflected in the shadows of cars and tall buildings as they flew by, outside my window.

A few moments later I heard 'K9-7' come from dispatch again followed by 'What's your 20?'

"Michael answered, "7th and Rochelle Avenue, ETA is a minute."

"Copy that K9-7. Be advised suspect's weapon is a possible AR-15 type."

"K9-7, 10-4." Michael replied. "Hold me 10-6 on the scene."

"10-4, K9-7, on the scene at 1420 hours," replied dispatch.

As Michael pulled around to the back alley I saw more officers with police vests and big guns slung around them on straps. I couldn't help barking a few times. I wasn't sure if it was a case of the nerves or I wanted to make my presence known. After all, I couldn't get out of the SUV and jibber-jab with them.

Michael stepped out and walked a few feet over to the officer with the most stripes on his sleeve. I listened through the SUV window that was open a few inches.

The sergeant shook Michael's hand and said, "Hey... Michael, congratulations on the K-9 squad. I'm jealous."

"Thanks, James," Michael replied. "What've we got going on here?"

"Bank hold up. We chased the suspect to a second floor apartment, apartment 211. Suspect fired a bunch of rounds on us with a semi-automatic, from the balcony out front. Sounds like an AR-15. I'd know for sure from a recent incident involving one. We've vacated the building along with the businesses across the front street. One officer said, he thought he might have seen a small boy's face for a moment at one of the windows in the back of the apartment.

I've got guys at both ends of the second floor hallway and Porter here," he nodded toward an officer standing close by, "has a big red key and if you want to force entry."

"Any info on who's on the apartment lease?" Michael inquired.

The sergeant pulled out a small notebook from his pocket. "A one, Phillip Aragon, served eight years at Leavenworth for armed robbery and multiple assaults, including one on a police officer, and ta-dah, paroled thirty-two days ago."

Michael nodded towards his cruiser. "I'll take Sirius up the back stairwell. Have the officers keep cover at the hallway ends. We'll try the easy way first. I'll grab a bullhorn and go up."

"Already done, Michael. Let me know if you need anything else."

"Roger that, James, thanks." Michael replied.

I watched Michael move towards me. He opened the door, hooked up the long line to my choke collar and fussed with my police vest for a second and said okay, boy, here we go. He grabbed a bullhorn out of a storage box on the floor of the backseat and we headed for the door to the back stairwell.

Officer Porter greeted us, at the door to the second floor corridor. The big red key sat next to him a few feet away.

Michael gave the other officer at the other end of the hallway a hand wave and received an acknowledgement back.

Michael pushed the microphone talk button on the mike attached to his vest. "K9-7, in position to make a K-9 entry announcement. Advise any units on the front side of the building to make an additional announcement for pending K-9 entry as well."

"10-4, K9-7." the dispatcher acknowledged. "Units stationed at the front side of K9-7's position, acknowledge."

Michael heard the front unit's affirmative replies.

Officer Porter along with Michael drew their guns, then Michael opened the stairwell door. He wedged it open with his foot so he could take a two handed firing stance, directly at the 211 apartment door.

I barked a few times, that's when Michael had me sit and calmed me down with a head rub.

Michael raised the bullhorn and directed it towards the middle of the hallway and 211. The bullhorn thundered, "Police K-9, come out now or I will send my dog! When my dog finds you, he will bite you!"

The same announcement went out through a cruiser's speaker out front, loud enough for Michael and Officer Porter to hear a faint echo of it in the building's interior.

Everyone waited and listened.

Michael's radio squawked, "Dispatch advises all units on the scene at 1414 West Dunaway Street go to TAC channel 8 at this time."

Michael switched to channel 8 and said, "K9-7 on 8." He heard the other units acknowledge their presence on the tactical frequency as well.

"K9-7, be advised that the suspect has stated via the balcony that he will release the child he's holding."

Michael acknowledged, "K9-7, copy. What's his deal?"

"K9-7, he wants no dog."

Michael radioed, "No deal. Let's wait and see if he lets him go anyway."

"K9-7," Sergeant Roland radioed, "reason for thinking he'll let the boy go?"

"I think he might be the suspect's son.

Apartment is in the suspect's name. Just a hunch, Sergeant."

"Okay, let's give it a few minutes, Corporal. Suspects not going anywhere anytime soon."

I began to grow impatient. I stood up and barked a few times. The sound echoed down the hallway. I'll bet the bad guy heard that.

Michael said, "Sit, easy, Sirius," and stroked my head.

I sat and waited again, trying to be patient for Michael. That is until I heard the door open and a little boy stepped out in the hallway rubbing his eyes. The door slammed closed again behind him.

Michael fixed his gunsight on the apartment door to give the boy cover as the officer at the other end of the hallway crept down the corridor towards the small child. The officer smiled at the boy and waved as he worked his way to him. The rescuing officer said a few words to the boy and took the child's hand in his. He led the boy back to the far-end stairwell.

My tail wagged away as I watched the boy walk towards safety.

Another officer came up the distant steps and walked the child down to freedom.

As soon as I saw the boy was safe I pulled at the long lead.

"K9-7, to all units," Michael radioed, "be advised the suspect has released the child. He is in safe custody. We are making forced entry now."

"Okay, Porter pick up the red key and follow me."

He snatched up the battering ram and I led Michael and Porter to 211. The officer at the other end of the hallway closed in and stationed himself on the other side of the door.

I sniffed the bottom of the door and barked. Michael calmed me down and with weapons drawn he nodded to Porter to use the red key.

Porter was a rather large officer and it only took one large swing of the big red key to mash the door open. The bang resounded throughout the empty hallway.

Michael shouted, "Police K-9" We entered the living room area and found no one, but I could smell the suspect's fresh scent in the room. With me on a lead, I sniffed my way to a closed back bedroom door. Michael, Porter, and the other officer from the far end hallway followed me with weapons drawn.

We positioned ourselves on each side of the closed door. Michael calmed me so I wouldn't bark and his final warning could be heard.

"Police K-9, come out now or I will send my dog. When my dog finds you, he will bite you. This is your final warning!"

We waited a few seconds for a reply then Michael nodded to Porter and he bashed the door open with the big red key.

I let out a barrage of barks that I had been holding back.

Michael looked in and scanned the room, but saw no one. He gave me the verbal release command and released the long lead on me.

I leapt into the room followed by, Michael, Porter, and the other officer. I started my sniff search.

Michael and the other officers checked the closet and under the bed and found no one.

I sniffed my way to an open window at the far end of the room. I raised myself up and barked out the broken window screen.

"K9-7, all units be advised, suspect is GOA, bailed out a south end window."

I heard a squad car loudspeaker outside say, "Aragon drop the weapon," followed by gun shots. Over Michael's radio I heard, "Suspect is on foot, armed, direction of the north wooded section of Swanson City Park. Suspect is white male, wearing a black sweatshirt, white tennis shoes, and a black baseball cap, armed with an AR-15 type weapon."

We ran outside and with the long lead, reattached, I kept my nose to the ground and picked up the suspect's trail. We started a run, following the scent.

Michael huffed the direction of pursuit on his microphone radio to dispatch. Several officers followed right behind us, panting as they ran to keep up. Marked units flashed their reds and blues as they moved down the park's adjacent streets.

I sensed the loud beating sound of a helicopter above. I was familiar with the sound it made from training exercises.

I increased my tracking pace even more, nose down, doing a snort, stiff, snort, stiff as I went. I was determined to find this robber before he could do anyone else any harm.

We entered a thicket of trees and brush. The scent lead to a large pine tree and the scent went up the trunk. I let out a barrage of barks at the suspect that was high up in the tree. Michael focused the aim of his gun sight on the suspect.

I wanted to scale that tree, but the best I could do was raise myself up on my hind legs and scratch the bark with my front paws.

"Drop your weapon and climb down, now!" Michael hollered upward to the guy. ...and don't drop it on my dog, toss it now!"

The two officers who had been behind us also had their guns drawn on the suspect.

I continued jumping against the base of the tree and gave it my, **'don't make me come up there'** bark and growl. I heard something hit the bushes nearby.

"I'm coming down... don't shoot!" the suspect hollered.

Michael pulled back on the long leash and made me sit and calmed me down as the suspect climbed down the pine.

"Get down on the ground, now! Face down, hands behind you and feet spread apart! Do it now!" Michael commanded as soon as the subject touched the ground.

One of the other officers cuffed him, read him his rights, and carted him off to a waiting squad car at the edge of the woods.

The officer remaining radioed the others and dispatch, that the suspect was in custody.

I got a big, 'good dog!' and two treats from Michael.

"You've got a special dog there, Corporal," the officer remaining stated as we walked out of the last part of the brush.

"Thanks, and thank you for the assist," Michael replied.

"My pleasure!" he replied. "Just glad to get another bad egg off the street."

"More like a rotten egg," Michael laughed.

"Yeah, no doubt." He grinned. He reached out and shook Michael's hand. I might want to look into that K-9 program when I lose my rookie status. I only have a year in. Take care."

"Do that," Michael stated. "Be safe."

"Well done, Sirius!" Michael said again while placing me back in the cruiser's back cubby. I got a couple of more pats and another treat, too! This work paid well!

TWENTY-FOUR

For me, that first day on street patrol would be an unforgettable one. It wasn't because of the calls we went on. I had found my calling in life.

I grew from a puppy to a young adult dog in a period of a little over a year. I recognized that the aging of a dog was different than the aging of a human. ...And from that quick period that had already passed me by, I knew that a dog's life was as fleeting as a shooting star.

Being aware of that in body and in spirit made a dog want to make a difference every day in someone's life, if it was possible.

I was startled out of a brief nap in the back of the cruiser after Michael flipped on the warbler siren. So... I'm not sure if I just dreamt about that stuff or thought it.

The engine noise climbed to a roar. I raised up and looked out the window. All I could see was a blur of row houses going by. It was getting kind of bouncy in the back section.

"Hang on, Sirius, be there in a minute!" Michael yelled over the noise as he weaved around traffic.

Dispatch transmitted, "All units responding to the 10-78, Dartmouth Avenue and Raines Street, officer needs assistance, can 10-22, cancel, at this time, suspect in custody. Cancel the officer assistance at 1600 hours."

"Looks like that call got resolved rather quickly, Sirius." Michael said. "You can relax, boy." Michael flicked off the siren and lights and slowed to the local traffic's speed.

"K9-7 is back, 10-8, dispatch." Michael transmitted.

"Copy that K9-7 at 1601 hours," the dispatcher replied.

Three other units en route also radioed communications that they were 10-8. I heard K9-1 go 10-8, and I heard my buddy, Jacob barking in the background. I barked in reply although it didn't get transmitted. I really looked up to that narc dog.

It wasn't long before the squad car radio squawked that it was 1700 hundred hours.

"One more hour till we get off, Sirius. What do you think about that, boy?"

I answered with a bark and just as I did, I heard, 'K9-7 what's your location?' come over the radio.

"K9-7, King Street and 99th," Michael answered.

"K9.7, meet officers for a commercial break-in with suspects still inside at Marcy's Warehouse service entrance, 997 Wharf Road."

"K9-7, copy, hold me en route," Michael replied.

"K9-7, at 1702 hours," dispatch replied.

As soon as I heard the K9-7, I stood up and looked at the view through the front windshield.

"So much for the getting off in an hour, Sirius," Michael said.

I tried not to show my enthusiasm about hearing dispatch say, K9-7, but my high-tail wag just gave me away.

We pulled up to another black and white parked sideways across the warehouse's service entrance. Its strobes flashed in every direction.

Michael lowered his window.

"Pearson, what-cha got?" Michael inquired."

"Hey, Michael. Congrats, on your new partner! I heard about you being back on the streets," Pearson stated.

"Thanks, he's the best partner I've ever had. He doesn't complain a lick," Michael replied.

"Ha... you've still got that 'chat 'em up humor', I see," Pearson replied.

"Yeah, sorry about the K-9 pun," Michael answered.

"We've got two held up inside confirmed by the owner's warehouse cameras. They shot two cameras out a couple of minutes ago. We've got units at all three entrances. Tried the loudspeaker several times with no response," Pearson stated.

"Oh, yeah, powers out in the area," Pearson added. It's pretty black in there. Guess the only thing that's on back-up power are the cameras. I'll move my vehicle."

"Got it, okay... we'll roll up to the break-in entrance," Michael replied.

"Anytime, appreciate the assist," Pearson replied. "Entrance three is the forced entry point. The last commercial break-in I was on didn't end well. One officer got shot. Lucky, though, she just got winged." Pearson nodded and moved his car so we could squeeze through onto the driveway, to the building.

We drove up to an entrance that had large number three over it. Michael stepped out and stood behind the driver's door, pointing his gun through the cruiser's open window at the entry point.

I heard Michael announce over the cruiser's PA, "Police K-9, come out now or I will send my dog. When my dog finds you, he will bite you."

The other units posted at the other doors echoed the same announcement on their loudspeakers.

We waited for several minutes for a response from within. When none came, Michael hooked up my six foot lead and we walked to the warehouse's door. Other officers that had recently arrived, provided fire cover for us.

Michael and I entered the semi-darkness of the warehouse inners. I smelled the smoke of gunpowder and I smelled the suspects. They were not close right now, but I could detect a trace of their scent that lingered in the air.

I sounded out my loudest bark in rapid succession. I liked that it echoed even louder in the massive building. We waited and listened. Hearing nothing, we crept forward with caution. It was growing darker as we went. Michael had his gun drawn and the two officers with us had their weapons out as well.

We paused and I let out a new series of warnings. Then we waited a few moments more.

I heard the crackling of cellophane wrap in the distance. I lead Michael and the other officers towards it.

I paused to take a few good whiffs of the air. I

detected two different odor sources and the smell of the gunpowder increased.

The scents I detected grew ever stronger as I prodded towards pallets of boxes stacked up high. We were near the middle of the warehouse when a gunshot went off. The bullet ricocheted off the cement floor, ten feet from me.

None of the guns in my training had ever spit out anything at me. It caused me to jump and that raised the hackles on my neck even more.

I looked up the instant I heard it and went into a barking frenzy. The suspects were on top of a box stack. Michael and the other officers fired their weapons, but the two men had already ducked down where we couldn't see them from ground level.

Michael pulled me back towards the shelter of a stack. The other two officers took cover at other stacks nearby. "Easy, boy... it's okay," Michael whispered to me. He gave me a rub behind my ears.

"Police! Throw down your weapons now!" Michael yelled up at the suspects.

We waited a few moments. I heard the clatter of metal on the concrete floor.

"Don't shoot!" One of the suspects shouted down. "We're coming down!"

"Do it now!" Michael commanded. "One at a time! No weapons!"

I heard another metallic sound of something else striking the cement, a large knife.

Michael and the other two officers watched as suspect one climbed down the stack.

I let out a series of barks.

Suspect one shouted as he neared the ground, "Please don't let your dog loose, please!"

"On the ground now, face down, hands where I can see them!" Michael commanded.

One officer handcuffed suspect number one. Michael and the other officer provided cover.

Suspect number two climbed down next.

"Down on the ground! Spread eagle!" Michael stated.

As soon as the two suspects were padded down for any other weapons they were informed of their arrest and Miranda rights.

"Which one of you fired the shot?" an officer asked.

"We've got nuthin' to say to you!" one suspect answered.

"I want my phone call!" the other suspect demanded. "Stupid-ass dog!"

The officers pulled the suspects to their feet, escorted them off to their cruiser's caged backseats and drove them to the station's jail.

Crime scene detectives showed up and bagged the two guns and the long knife.

Michael and I left the warehouse after the owner showed up and secured the warehouse. Before the owner left he thanked us numerous times. He said, I was a handsome dog and gave me a pat on the head. I appreciated that.

After Michael filed the necessary paperwork we went 10-7, out of service. I was police dog-tired, too.

TWENTY-FIVE

Michael and I arrived home late. Jenny and Jasper had already gone to bed. Pam was still up and gave us both hugs and kisses.

"I was starting to get concerned," Pam said to Michael. "Don't forget to slip me a text once in a while, just so I'll know my corporal and his dog are good."

"Sorry, Pam," Michael replied. "I lost all track of time today. Crazy day! What's for supper?"

"Ah... now I've got my man back." Pam smiled. "One of your favorites, beef stew," She answered. "Are you ready or do you want to chill for a bit first?"

"Let's sit on the back porch for a while first," Michael replied. "Everything good with the kids today?"

"Well let's get comfy on the porch and I'll tell you, Honey," Pam answered.

We all moseyed out to what I had started to think of as the playground and dog park. Michael and Pam had it looking pretty similar. The kids loved it and so did I.

"Well," Pam said, "Jasper went to the school nurse today complaining of a sore throat. I picked him up early and a little ice cream on the way home made it go away. His throat wasn't red—no temperature, so it was that miracle chocolate frozen concoction again that cured him," she laughed.

"Ah, yes, works wonders. Chocolate, the miracle drug," Michael smiled in agreement."

"... and Jenny?" Michael inquired.

"She's good. She's got some drawings from class that she can't wait to show you. One of them is of you and Sirius. Mrs. Perkins gave her a gold star for that one. You're going to love it," she smiled.

"Can't wait to see them," Michael replied. "Oh, I remember the rule from her last showing. 'These aren't drawings, Daddy, they're art,' she said."

"I almost slipped and called them drawings, but I caught myself just in time," Pam stated. "She's a pretty good little artist."

"Like her mother," Michael added.

I saw Michael put his hand on hers and kiss. I knew that this was my chance to slip in the doggie door and steal upstairs to see the kids. I could move quickly even after a long, hard day.

When I arrived upstairs, Jenny was sound asleep.

"Sirius... boy... you're home... " Jasper said in a semi-whisper. I padded over to him for a big hug and kiss. I give him a dog kiss and could smell chocolate ice cream.

I hopped up on the foot of Jasper's bed and fell dead asleep until morning.

The morning light wasn't even dancing on the floor yet when Michael and I ventured out for another day as K9-7.

TWENTY-SIX

The first hour of our patrol was uneventful and my intuition sweep over me in waves. I was a firm believer in a dog's gifts. Dog's had no real track of time, but we could sense an illness in its form. Things like low blood sugar in a diabetic human or even a seizure coming on before any physical signs appeared. I could sense someone's mood from a sniff or turn my nose up at bad water even before tasting it.

I sensed a wicked day was forthcoming. It was today... ...not sure what that meant yet, but it...

"K9-7," what's your location?" the dispatcher asked.

"K9-7, Howard Road and 22nd Avenue," Michael answered.

"K9-7, the dispatcher stated, "phone-in report of a bomb onboard an inbound passenger train, arriving in ten minutes at Downtown Metro Station. See the station manager, Emmanuel Cohen."

"K9-7, copy, en-route," Michael replied.

"Hang on Sirius!" Michael told me. The cruiser's siren began warbling. A throaty mechanical roar came from the front of the cruiser and the scenery flashed past my window.

"K9-7, what's your ETA?" dispatch queried.

"K9-7, five minutes," Michael answered.

"K9-7, Copy. See the conductor-in chief, Cyrus Parker, once onboard the train."

"Copy, K9-7," Michael replied.

When we sped-in to the train station, Michael went in to talk to the station manager and I stayed behind. I was a little riled up from the fast, siren-blaring ride here and barked at a few passersby's that passed close by to the cruiser.

Six other police vehicles showed up along with the fire department. The police officers met Michael just outside our car.

"Hey, Michael," one of the officers greeted Michael with a handshake. "Any additional info, yet?"

"Long time, no see, Pearson," Michael replied. "Yeah, station manager say's train is two minutes out, arriving from the east. He says the train didn't dead stop to evacuate due to it being the monthly discount day for seniors. Lots of seniors on board and it's a frigid 20 degrees out. Call it a judgement call."

"Yeah," Pearson said, "... and it would of taken thirty minutes longer for us to reach the train through the east marsh area if it had stopped."

"I want you to spread yourselves on the train's exit doors to assist passengers if needed," Michael instructed the other officers. "I'll take my dog, Sirius and start searching the train as soon as the train is evacuated."

I heard them continue to talk together. I wanted to get out of this vehicle now and go hunt. I had heard the word, 'bomb' and knew what it meant to me.

"Passengers haven't been notified," Michael stated. "Manager said, the conductor didn't want to create a panic stampede getting off the train. Train conductor announced a two-hour delay for emergency train maintenance and instructed everyone to disembark immediately at the station."

The fellow officers walked off towards the train platform and Michael hooked up my short lead and brought me out of the cruiser. Finally!

We headed over to the rails just as the train pulled into the station. I had never been on a train before. It looked huge, but I reasoned that it was not as large a search for a bomb as a warehouse full of stuff.

I watched the train personnel as they tried to coax the people off faster. They told them, 'The sooner we get everyone off, the faster we can get the maintenance done and get back underway.'

While we waited, Michael said to me or maybe to himself, "Yeah... there won't be any maintenance, if there's no train."

Once everyone was off and a safe distance away, Michael and I went on board. Michael took me off the short leash and gave me the search bomb command.

I went to work doing my search for bomb component smells using my snort, stiff, snort, snort, stiff, scent detection method.

I scoured three passenger cars with Michael following close behind me. When we entered the next car, towards the middle of the train, I detected a bomb material, tetryl. My olfactory snoot cells were on overdrive.

I paused at a middle seat with a sweatshirt on it. What I was looking for was underneath the shirt. I remembered from my training not to nose a potential explosive smelling item. I sat down and waited for Michael.

"Good dog, Sirius!" Michael said, and gave me one of my favorite treats.

"K9-7, dispatch," Michael said, over his uniform mike attachment.

"K9-7, go," the dispatch acknowledged.

"K9-7, requesting the bomb robot. Passenger car number 1711, track 4."

"K9-7, to confirm, a bomb found?" dispatch asked.

"10-4, a possible bomb, middle seat on the station side," Michael stated. He and Sirius headed out of the car, cordoned off the area with police tape and waited.

The other officers having heard the call to dispatch helped place the tape and secure the immediate area. They gathered around Michael to ask what he had found.

The robot and its operator showed up a few minutes later. In the meantime, train personnel had decoupled the train cars on both sides of car 1711, and moved them. Car 1711 now sat alone on the track.

I watched from a distance as the officer placed his robot at the top of the steps of car 1711, then he quickly retreated to stare at a square that he held in his hands.

A few minutes later everything around me flashed and thunder radiated from the train platform. Through the smoke, I saw that car 1711 was now only a mass of twisted wreckage.

I had a ringing sensation in my ears and some of the officers that were closest to the blast were bent over with their hands over their ears. Michael and the other officers went over to assist and several ambulances standing by pulled up.

Michael checked me over, too. He drove me to the vet's office that I had visited before for police check-ups and shots. If I had to choose I think I preferred the explosion to the temperature check and probing.

I checked out okay as did all of the other officers. No lives were lost and no one was permanently injured. My intuition had been right about a wicked day and I heeded it whenever it spoke to me from that day forward.

TWENTY-SEVEN

I always knew this; a dog's life was as fleeting as a shooting star. Years sped by answering calls on the streets where a police dog was needed. I had started to gray a bit around the muzzle. It matched a few gray hairs I noticed on Michael's head, too.

The mean streets were no friend of mine, but there had been plenty of good people to rescue off of them. For that I was grateful. Gratifying to be of purpose, my treat to the world.

I thought back on the armed burglary suspect, who held a young family at bay, that is until Michael and I disarmed and captured him.

I remember a little girl who was kidnapped. That girl reminded me of my Jenny, safe at home. I tracked the kidnapper for hours through some harsh terrain. Finally after Michael and I tipped toward exhaustion, we located the kidnapper and the girl in a desolate cabin in the foothills.

With special ops surrounding the cabin and a helicopter circling above, the kidnapper surrendered. The girl was rescued and checked out okay at the hospital. The other officers at the scene asked Michael if my tail always wagged so much. Michael laughed and said, 'Only when he's successfully saved someone.'

Now... that was somewhat true, however finding

that little girl safe made my tail wag extra and I couldn't seem to stop it that day.

There were many good memories like that. There was also a painful memory that might end my career as a K-9 officer that brings us to this day.

Today... I was shot three times by a wanted fugitive, wanted for murder. He held fifteen children hostage at his ex-wife's daycare center.

As I lay in the intensive care unit of the veterinary animal hospital, I couldn't think of anything except the pain, until the vet gave me a second morphine shot. Then half in conscious and half out, my life replayed in my head like a movie.

I heard Michael's voice and could kind of see his face go in and out of focus.

"Sirius, hang in there boy," he said. "You are one brave dog, all the kids are safe." He gently stroked me behind my ear then he bent over to kiss my head.

Michael wasn't a head kisser like I've seen some other dog owners do. They would bend over and kiss their dogs' head a lot. But I was thankful for his constant touch and I needed that one special kiss he had given me right now.

I heard the vet say, "Michael, we need to get this surgery underway. I'll send word to you as soon as I know anything further. Might be a while."

I heard Michael sigh.

"There's nothing you can do right now," the vet assured him. "You can go home and get a little rest if you want."

"I'll be in the waiting room," Michael answered.

"Might be all afternoon, Michael," the doc said, placing a hand on Michael's shoulder.

"I can't leave right now," Michael replied. "Thanks, Doc, I'll be in the lobby."

"I understand," the doc replied. "We'll do our best. I want you to know upfront, it's a 50/50 chance of success."

"Thank you, Doc." I heard Michael say. It sounded like he was a long ways away. Their voices were starting to fade in and out. He gave me one final ear stroke and turned and walked out. That's the last thing I remembered as darkness closed in all around me.

In the lobby, Michael was soon joined by Pam, Jenny, and Jasper. Five other police officers came in and sat with them.

"Daddy, will Sirius please be able to come home today?" Jenny pleaded. She placed her small hands in his.

The waiting room grew quiet as she waited for her father's answer.

"Not today, Honey," Michael answered. "I wish he could."

"Me, too," Jasper added.

Pam noticed a tear run down Michael's face. She had seen his tears only a few times before, when the kids were born, after his mother died, and the day he wore the black tape over his badge for his best friend, Officer James Jamison, who was killed in the line of duty last year.

"We all want Sirius home soon," one of the officer's present said. He pulled two lollipops from his shirt pocket and handed one each to Jenny and

Jasper.

Michael brightened when he saw that. Lollipop, which was Officer Gunston's nickname, always carried lollipops to give to kids in stressful situations on his calls. He had been doing it for as long as anyone could remember.

Jasper and Jenny smiled and reached for the suckers and thanked him.

Around five o'clock, after several hours had gone by, Lollipop pulled a notepad from his other shirt pocket and announced that he was making a pizza run. He took everyone's orders and headed out the door.

Officer Miller from the police K-9 academy was coming in the door and held the door open for Lollipop's exit. Lollipop knew Miller's penchant for being a bully, but he always tried to see the good side of everyone regardless.

"Hey, Lollipop," Miller greeted him as he walked in. "Looks like a police convention with all the cruisers outside"

"Hey, Chet Miller, haven't seen you in ages," Lollipop replied. "What's shaken?"

"Nuthin, Lolli, and you?" Miller asked.

"Going on a pizza run for the gang, want anything?" Lollipop asked.

"Sure, appreciate you." Miller answered. "How about a medium pepperoni? I'm buying." He fished out two one-hundred dollar bills from his wallet.

Lollipop tried to hide his look of astonishment when he saw Miller's gesture.

"Yes sir, be back in a flash," Lollipop stated. He

headed for his car still wondering in his head what had gotten into Miller. Miller never went out of his way for anyone, he thought.

"Don't look now," one of the other officers in the lobby said to the others, but bulldozer Miller approaches."

Miller greeted everyone then strode over to Michael.

"Sorry to hear about, Sirius, Michael," Miller stated. "I want you to know I was wrong about him—his size and all. I've been wrong about a lot of things. Turning a new leaf. Hope it's not too late for me." He held out his hand. "Friends?" he asked.

Michael stood. He reached out and shook Miller's hand. "Friends," he said.

"How's Sirius doing?" Miller asked.

"He's still in surgery and doc gives him 50/50 of pulling through." Michael replied and sat back down.

Upon seeing Miller shake Michael's hand and hearing his sentiment, one of the other officers said, "That's the best thing that's happened today." He stood and reached to shake Miller's hand. A few other officer's did as well, however a few reserved judgement for later.

Miller gave Michael a reassuring pat on the shoulder and sat down next to him.

I was starting to come to. I still had an oxygen mask over my snout when I had the strangest dream. I smelled Officer Miller nearby. I dreamt that Office Miller was now working as a greeter at a local pet warehouse. He was handing out dog biscuits, smiling, as each dog strode in the front door. The really strange part was that he still had his police uniform on.

I also thought I smelled pizza. Then a sharp pain came over me and everything went black again.

"Pizza pies are here!" Lollipop said, as he came reeling in the front door with a large stack of pizza boxes.

"I saw a newscast at the pizza place while I was there. Seems that Sirius is all over the news. The kids he saved were on the tube thanking him and wishing him well. It was something to watch!"

The officers ate lightly and shared the pies with the hospital staff who brought out sodas from the back room frig.

The vet came out just as everyone was finishing up. He stood in front of the group and paused before he spoke.

"Is he Sirius's dog doctor, Daddy?" Jenny asked.

"Yes, he is Sweetie." Michael answered. "Let's listen and see what he has to say."

"Hi, folks," the vet said. "Sirius is one tough dog, he's been through a major trauma that in my twenty years of practice I don't think most dogs would have survived.

"Sirius is stable. The next few days for him are critical for his recovery. I found that his vest stopped what I think would have been a fatal shot. One round penetrated the vest lodging in the lung/chest area. It missed the heart and the liver. I was able to remove it. I don't think they'll be any permanent damage there. The two rounds in the right hip, I'm afraid are going to give Sirius an early retirement on disability. He'll walk again, but running is out of the question.

"May I suggest that we savor the good news, and I'm sorry about the bad news," he concluded.

"Can we see him?" Michael asked.

"Michael, you and family first," the doc answered. "Then anyone else that wants to see Sirius, one at a time, please, but only for a minute. He's groggy and still coming out of sedation."

Michael, Pam, Jasper, and Jenny filed into the back intensive care room.

Michael and the children gently petted Sirius's head.

Pam bent down and spoke to him. "My, Sirius... The kids you saved at the day care were on TV thanking you. You are a hero! You've always been a hero." She kissed him on his head.

"Okay, gang, we better go and let Sirius get some rest," Michael said.

"Bye, Sirius, we love you," Jenny said, as a tear ran down her face.

"Don't cry," Jasper said. "Sirius is going to be alright." He hugged his sister and they all walked together back out to the waiting room.

Officer Miller saw Lollipop standing by the door to see Sirius. He was next in line.

When Michael and family exited the door back into the waiting room, Officer Miller said, "Michael, can I be next to see Sirius, I'm still on duty and my meal break should be up by now."

"Lollipop?" Michael questioned.

"Sure, Go ahead Miller," Lollipop replied.

"Thanks," Miller said, patting Lollipop on the

shoulder.

Miller entered and stood next to Sirius. He stroked Sirius's head.

"Sirius, I'm sorry that I was so mean to you. I was wrong. You are one of the best K-9 officers to ever grace the academy."

The crazy dreams with Officer Miller were back. I opened my eyes half way and look up trying to focus. It was Miller.

With my tail extending halfway out from the blanket I was under, I managed one wag. I saw Miller smile for the first time that I can remember.

"Get well, Sirius," Miller said. "I'll tell Michael to call me if you need anything." He turned and left.

Michael, Pam, and the kids thanked the vet who operated on Sirius and headed home in the nightfall.

On the drive home, Michael asked, "Did you hear what Miller told me just before we left, Pam?"

"No, what did he say?" Pam inquired.

"He said, to call him if we needed anything," Michael replied.

"From what you've told me about Officer Miller, I sure didn't expect that," Pam stated.

"Remember, Garcia who works with Miller in K-9 training?" Michael asked Pam.

"Yeah, of course. She was Sirius's main handler in his training," she replied.

"Just before we left the vet's," Michael explained, "Garcia told me her child was one of the kid's held hostage at the day care ...and Miller's daughter, Megan was there, too."

"You're kidding. Wow!" Pam exclaimed.

"Megan was the kid the gunman held as a shield." Michael said.

"Poor kid, poor Miller..." Pam replied.

"Yeah, but Sirius got hold of the gunman's arm long enough for Megan to get away, except the guy picked up the gun with his other free hand and shot Sirius. That's when we got a bead on the gunman and opened fire on him."

"The children are probably traumatized by now." Pam surmised.

"Unfortunately, but they're alive thanks to Sirius," Michael answered.

TWENTY-EIGHT

Michael's phone rang before daylight filtered through the curtains.

"Michael are you awake?" Pam asked. "Get that, it might be the vet's."

Michael grabbed his phone off the nightstand and looked at the screen. "Wrong number, don't know anyone from Hartford, Connecticut. It's 7 a.m., vet's open. I'm calling the vet's."

As Michael waited for the animal hospital to pick up.

"Put them on the speaker, Michael".

"Hollister Animal Hospital," the receptionist answered cheerfully.

Michael sensed that someone slept well last night. "Hi, I'm calling about Sirius, this is Officer Collins."

"Mr. Collins, hold please. I'll put you through to Doctor Hollister."

"Thank you," Michael replied.

"You're welcome, and thank you for rescuing the children yesterday. One of them was my neighbor's child."

"Welcome, Sirius saved them though," Michael answered.

"Thank you, both. Okay, hold the line, sir," she replied.

Pam patted Michael on the shoulder and kissed his cheek.

"Hi, Michael," Doc Hollister answered. "Sirius is stable. He had a seizure last night which is probably due to his injuries. His vitals have stabilized and are approaching normal."

"Thanks, Doc! That's a relief," Michael stated.

"Thank you, Doc Hollister!" Pam said loud enough for her to be heard in the background.

"You are welcome," Doc replied. "Michael, you and your family are welcome to see him anytime, but no other visitors for now. I had to run off a bunch of reporters this morning. I gave them a briefing, but then they wanted to take a picture of Sirius. Guess I can't blame them. He's a celebrity."

"Yeah, I guess it goes with the territory," Michael replied.

"Sure does," the vet stated. "Any questions right now?"

"Are the seizures temporary?" Michael questioned.

"They should dissipate on his road to recovery," Doc answered.

"Good to hear." Michael said. "Okay, I'll let you go, Doc. Thanks again."

"Okay," Doc replied, "then I'll talk with you later, bye."

"Well, so far, so good," Michael stated.

"I'll make breakfast and then we'll get dressed and head down to the see Sirius," Pam said.

"No, I'll make breakfast, Sweetie." Michael said. "Besides I need something to do since I'm on administrative leave with pay until the department finishes their investigation of the shooting."

"I'll let you, Honeybunch" Pam smiled. "I'll go turn the table on the kids and wake them up for a change," she said with a giggle."

Pam led Jasper and Jenny down to the kitchen. Pam whispered in Michael's ear, "As soon as they opened their eyes they both asked about Sirius. They really, really love that dog!"

"I know, Honey. We all do," Michael replied. "Breakfast is ready. Have a seat, everyone and I will serve it up!"

Jenny sat at the table and watched everyone eat. Soon Jasper stopped eating and just starred at his sister with his lower lip poked out.

"Honey, what's wrong?" Pam asked Jenny.

"Are we going to get to see Sirius, today, Mommy? Please..."

"Of course we are," she answered. "Right after you eat all of your breakfast. You, too, Jasper."

Jenny's face brightened. "Good!" She exclaimed.

"I'm finishing all mine fast!" Jasper stated in a loud voice.

"Me, too!" Jenny said.

"Not too fast, kids," Michael instructed. "Chew your food and enjoy it. I worked hard to make it for you."

"Okay, Daddy," Jasper answered. "Thank you."

"You are both welcome," Michael replied. "It has love in it."

"Yuk," Jasper, said. "It tastes different."

Michael and Pam laughed.

"Nooo!" Jenny said. "Daddy means he made it

because he likes you. It's the same eggs..."

"It's good, Daddy. I guess I'm not hungry," Jasper said. "I'm worried about Sirius, Is he gonna get breakfast, too?"

"Eat what you can," Michael replied. "The hospital will take very good care of Sirius. He'll get breakfast."

As soon as the kids excused themselves from the table, they ran upstairs to get dressed.

Pam shouted after them, "Don't forget to brush your teeth."

They both shouted, "Okay, Mommy!"

When they arrived at the animal hospital, Dr. Hollister came out to see them.

"Sirius is progressing well. No more seizures since last night. He ate a little soft food and water this morning. That's a good sign. But, we'll keep him on the IV's for a few days. Any questions?"

"Not right now, can we see him?" Michael asked.

"Right this way" He led them to the back intensive care ward. "We had to donate all the flowers people sent. My staff was sneezing and so were the animals. The last time I saw so many flowers was at the Rose Parade," Doc stated with a chuckle.

"Nice," Michael replied.

Sirius lay on his side. He moved his gaze up towards his visitors and gave a small tail wag.

"Hey, boy. How are you feelings? A bit rough, I know," Michael said to him. He bent down to peck a kiss on his head.

Jenny and Jasper stroked Sirius's head.

Pam waited for them to step back, so as not to

crowd him.

"Can I sign his cast?" Jasper questioned. He looked at the white cast that covered Sirius's rear right leg up to his hip.

"Not right now," Pam answered as she scratched gently behind Sirius's ear.

"We'll be back this afternoon," Michael told the receptionist before they left.

Dr. Hollister said I made remarkable progress in the days and weeks that followed.

I looked forward to Michael and Pam's visits twice a day. The kids came to see me once-a-day on school days, but always twice-a-day on weekends. When the kids were present, I managed to give them extra tails wags and kisses.

My family's visits made me more determined to return to them sooner than later.

I was finally back on solid food. Thank goodness, the mush they had been giving me was tasty, but left me wanting more.

After one of my family's visits, the doc told them that they could finally take me home.

Then, with help and some physical therapy home visits from a traveling therapist named, Trish, I was able to stand and step by step, walk normally once more after the cast came off.

I had a crush on Trish. I could smell other dog scents on her when she arrived each morning. She either had another patient like me, somewhere or a dog like me. I knew it.

TWENTY-NINE

I spent a lot of time sprawled out on the back patio, the sun helped me to heal and gave me peace.

Michael went back to work and told me that he was working on temporary assignment at the K-9 training police academy. I stayed home. I could fast walk now across the yard with the kids, but my running days were over. I winded kind of easy, too, and my tongue hung out way too often.

I didn't mind. I was just glad to walk again. I didn't mind staying home with the kids and Pam either. Although, on the days when the kids were in school, I had too much time to sit around. My thoughts wandered as to the assistance I could be, back on patrol, helping people and keeping Michael safe.

On a few of those days, when the kids were in school, and I started to mope around, Pam would take me to the dog park. It was nice mingling with my brothers and sisters.

Michael came home one day and said to Pam, "Sirius's retirement party is tomorrow at the academy. The mayor and police chief are going to be there. One of our state senator's will even be there as a keynote speaker, along just about everybody that doesn't have to pull duty tomorrow."

"That's fantastic! I'm glad that they're recognizing Sirius's service," Pam replied.

"That's not all," Michael added, "Apparently, Time Magazine somehow got wind of the story about Sirius's heroics, maybe from the city paper. I'm not sure, anyway, they want to do an article on Sirius."

"Wow! That is so cool!" Pam exclaimed. "What time is the event? You're off, right?"

"I wouldn't miss it if I wasn't off." Michael chuckled. "I'd have to investigate an anonymous report called in by you, Pam, of a loud party complaint at the police academy." Michael laughed again.

"This is exciting and sad all at the same time," Pam said with a frown.

"It is," Michael agreed, "but it sure is a good way to go out if you have to."

Trish, the traveling dog physical therapist, paid her weekly visits to our home. After each session I was a little sore. I could accept the trade-off because each week I made some progress. Besides she wore the right perfume, dog scents.

The next day at the celebration would always stay with me, pictured in my mind's eye. Maybe, it was because of the many bright flash photos that were taken.

I sat on a red carpet surrounded by my fellow K-9 officers. Our handlers sat behind us. We all wore our police K-9 vests with the badge patches. It felt good to wear it one last time. My old pal, Jacob who had retired a few years back sat next to me.

I didn't understand much of the dignitary's speeches except I knew they were good because everyone kept interrupting by clapping.

I did hear the police chief say, 'K9-7' and the word, 'retired' together. That's when Michael bent over and whispered in my ear, "Hey, Sirius, your call sign is being retired in your honor. That's a first, buddy!"

I nosed up and gave Michael a lick on the chin. That had been one of those special moments. You know, the kind of day where you can still picture it in your head. It's forever present.

The house was quiet that night after the sun stopped peering in the windows. Everyone was pretty much exhausted.

The next day I noticed that Michael placed a group picture of all of us, from yesterday, on the fireplace mantle shelf. There's a large footstool in front of the fireplace. It's now my roost for seeing the photo close up at least once a day.

After breakfast, we hopped in the car and headed for 'someplace special' according to Michael.

Michael had told me yesterday that he had a big surprise for me today. I don't know what it could be, except I couldn't imagine it being any greater than my retirement tribute.

THIRTY

I sat between Jenny and Jasper in the backseat watching the scenery go by. We passed tall buildings that were soon replaced by trees stretching up to the blue sky. Next, clouds of dust rolled by the windows and the ride got bumpy. I began to detect a familiar scent coming from outside the car. It was the smell of the farm I was raised on.

I was so excited, but Jenny wasn't because she was getting beat with the increasing velocity of my tail wag.

"Sirius, sit down," Jenny said giggling.

Sirius is beating you up with his tail," Jasper teased.

"I know, "Jenny replied.

As they pulled up to the farmyard gate, Jasper asked, "Is this where Sirius was born, Mommy?"

"It sure is! That's his Mommy standing right there," Pam pointed at her.

Sure enough there was Mother with her snout stuck out between the gate slates.

Michael opened my door and I ran over to her to exchange greetings as best I could through the gate.

Monty came out of the farmhouse and opened the gate. "Welcome home, Sirius!" He bent down and hugged me.

I nuzzled Mother and felt her warmth once again. It seemed like it had been a lifetime since I had seen her... and in dog's years maybe it had.

"Look, Michael, at the banner on the porch railing," Pam said.

Jenny read it out loud. "Welcome Home, Sirius, Pup!"

"You're puppy home, Sirius," Jasper laughed.

We walked to the porch steps and the farmhouse door opened.

Out came, big brother, Nova and my sisters, Celeste and Calypso.

My brother and sisters looked the same as the vision I had on the night of the shooting. They all had appeared to me out of the darkness, when I had the seizure at the animal hospital.

We nuzzled and dog kissed each other until Mother got in the middle of us and got all the attention lavished on her. She deserved it.

All afternoon we played ball and watched the chickens dance. None of us tried to chase them any longer. Finally, we positioned ourselves next to each other for a nap on the porch in the warmth of the afternoon sun.

At the turn of each new season, Michael, Pam, and the kids would bring me to the farm for another gathering, in what would become a joyous four-times-a-year reuniting.

My Michael was promoted to a sergeant and was now head of K-9 training. Officer Garcia, I mean, Corporal Garcia, now, was his assistant. Officer Miller who had kept his word on turning a new leaf, finally made corporal and was the senior community relations officer. Imagine that!

Lollipop... well... Lollipop was Lollipop. He retired and started two shelters, one for displaced families and one for animals. That gentle soul had more to give than ol' Saint Nick!

My old pal, Jacob paid us a welcome visit at home once in a while. Even though he was older than me, he kept me young with his backyard ball-catching antics.

My journey, has been a dog's life, extraordinaire.

My heart and soul told me though, that it was my brother and sister's lives that filled me with pride the most. They each had served their masters separately as therapy, mobility assistance, and guide dogs. I felt their love returned to me three-fold.

I was lucky, alright, that's for sure, to be their brother.

About The Author

What may have created the desire for Mark Enlow to lean towards the creative side of life might have started with the clay model of a dog that to his astonishment was show-cased in the glass hall showcase in elementary school. ...or maybe it was later when a short story written in college and given accolades by his English professor fanned the humble flames of an authorship path.

Mark said, "Yes, that was it!"

It's the journey to a foreign place, the surprise discovery, an unexpected laugh, a lovable character, or a sudden twist of the story that are some of the elements that Mark enjoys creating for his readers.

You can visit Mark's website at,
https://markenlowauthor.com
and on X (formerly Twitter) at,
https://x.com/markenlowauthor
(A sign-in to your X account might be necessary to view Mark's posts.)

Oh... he asked me to give you this note:

Today, readers depend a lot on reviews. So, in order for others to discover this book, could you please give your feedback for this book on Amazon.com/Stand Proud and Bark? Thank you for reading the story!

Also by Mark Enlow,

'The King of Zu Island' can also be found on Amazom.com. Here's a brief peek:

A hurricane, a mysterious island, chatty animals, gnomes, a mermaid, a king, and some very wicked pirates come to life in a page-turning fantasy/adventure story for young readers ages 8-12.